"I'll think about your proposal."

"You do that," Judah said, "and don't forget to tell the good doc your business merger's off." He crossed to the door, putting his hand out to open it for her—at least that's what she thought he was going to do—before pressing his lips against her cheek, his stubble grazing her ever so slightly. "Just so you know, Darla, I don't plan on mixing business with my marriage."

His meaning was unmistakable. His hand moved to her waist in a possessive motion, lingering at her hip just for a second, capturing her. She remembered everything—how good he'd made her feel, how magical a night was in his arms—and wished his proposal was made from love and not possessiveness.

Judah pulled the door open. "Next time I see you will be at the altar."

Dear Reader,

I hope Creed's story made its way to your keeper shelf! With the third installment of the *Callahan Cowboys,* Judah Callahan gets set to avoid Aunt Fiona's matchmaking, Bode Jenkins's scheming, his brothers' mischief and anyone else who might think about pressing him toward the altar. Judah would secretly love to win Rancho Diablo, if only he didn't have to marry to get it! But when he finds his dream girl, Darla Cameron, naked in his bed, Judah's determination to stay away from all women wavers. It's just too hard to stay away from the wedding shop owner and his own heart's desire.

As school begins and carpool lines form and fall starts to tease us with football and cooler weather, let's watch Judah "suffer" the joys of home life and earn the love of a good woman in *The Bull Rider's Twins.* It promises to be a season he'll enjoy—even if he doesn't realize it right away. So here's to the mystical, wild Diablos at Rancho Diablo, and to joy in your own corner of the world.

All my best,

Tina

www.tinaleonard.com

twitter.com/tina_leonard

facebook.com/tinaleonardbooks

The Bull Rider's Twins

TINA LEONARD

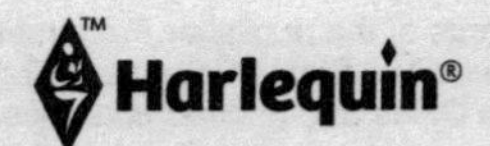

TORONTO NEW YORK LONDON
AMSTERDAM PARIS SYDNEY HAMBURG
STOCKHOLM ATHENS TOKYO MILAN MADRID
PRAGUE WARSAW BUDAPEST AUCKLAND

Recycling programs for this product may not exist in your area.

ISBN-13: 978-0-373-75374-1

THE BULL RIDER'S TWINS

This edition published by arrangement with Harlequin Books S.A.

For questions and comments about the quality of this book please contact us at Customer_eCare@Harlequin.ca

www.Harlequin.com

Printed in U.S.A.

ABOUT THE AUTHOR

Tina Leonard is a bestselling author of more than forty projects, including a popular thirteen-book miniseries for Harlequin American Romance. Her books have made the Waldenbooks, Ingram and Nielsen BookScan bestseller lists. Tina feels she has been blessed with a fertile imagination and quick typing skills, excellent editors and a family who loves her career. Born on a military base, she lived in many states before eventually marrying the boy who did her crayon printing for her in the first grade. Tina believes happy endings are a wonderful part of a good life. You can visit her at www.tinaleonard.com.

Books by Tina Leonard

HARLEQUIN AMERICAN ROMANCE

977—FRISCO JOE'S FIANCÉE‡‡
981—LAREDO'S SASSY SWEETHEART‡‡
986—RANGER'S WILD WOMAN‡‡
989—TEX TIMES TEN‡‡
1018—FANNIN'S FLAME‡‡
1037—NAVARRO OR NOT‡‡
1045—CATCHING CALHOUN‡‡
1053—ARCHER'S ANGELS‡‡
1069—BELONGING TO BANDERA‡‡
1083—CROCKETT'S SEDUCTION‡‡
1107—LAST'S TEMPTATION‡‡
1113—MASON'S MARRIAGE‡‡
1129—MY BABY, MY BRIDE*
1137—THE CHRISTMAS TWINS*
1153—HER SECRET SONS*
1213—TEXAS LULLABY**
1241—THE TEXAS RANGER'S TWINS**
1246—THE SECRET AGENT'S SURPRISES**
1250—THE TRIPLETS' RODEO MAN**
1263—THE TEXAS TWINS
1282—THE COWBOY FROM CHRISTMAS PAST
1354—THE COWBOY'S TRIPLETS‡
1362—THE COWBOY'S BONUS BABY‡

‡‡Cowboys by the Dozen
* The Tulips Saloon
** The Morgan Men
‡ Callahan Cowboys

Many thanks to my editor Kathleen Scheibling, for believing in this series, always having faith in me and editing my work with a sure hand.

There are many people at Harlequin who make my books ready for publication, most of whom I will never have the chance to thank in person, and they have my heartfelt gratitude.

Also many thanks to my children, who by now are both off to college, leaving me with an empty nest. It's not hard to envision me writing a series about babies—I had an extremely blessed experience with my two kids, and I thank you for your faith and encouragement.

And many, many thanks to the very generous readers who are the reason for my success. I could not write without your caring words and loyal support.

Chapter One

"Judah is my seeker," Molly Callahan said of her toddler son, to which her husband, Jeremiah, replied, "Then the apple didn't fall far from the tree, my love."

Judah Callahan couldn't believe the woman of his dreams was waiting in his bed. Unless he missed his guess, Darla Cameron was as naked as the day she was born.

"I've been waiting for you," she said, sitting up and holding the sheet to her chest. His throat went dry as a bone in a New Mexico desert. Blond hair cascaded over pale shoulders, and big blue eyes gazed at him with apprehension. She was nervous, Judah realized, closing the door and locking it behind him.

He wanted to say he'd been waiting for her for years. "I'd think you'd been in the champagne, but I noticed you didn't go near it except to toast Creed and Aberdeen."

She shook her head. "It was a lovely wedding. Really beautiful. All the valentine decorations were so romantic."

He couldn't take his eyes off her. Whatever she thought was romantic about Creed's wedding was nowhere near as attractive as Darla showing up nude in his bed. A little worry crossed her face, and he realized she was afraid he might turn down what she was obviously offering.

Not a chance.

He seated himself on the foot of the bed, the sight of her creamy skin setting him on fire. "If not an excess of champagne, why tonight?"

She blushed. "I wish I could tell you."

That didn't sound like the Darla he knew. Darla was forthright. An excellent businesswoman—her new calling since she'd hung up her nurse's badge and gone into business as wedding shop owner with Jackie Samuels. "Try."

She shook her head. "Be with me."

He wasn't going to put her, or himself, through any more agony. He kissed Darla, amazed at the sweet taste of her. "Peaches," he said, his mind fogging up. "I always wondered what you smelled like, and now I know. You even taste like peaches."

She moved his hand to the sheet, and he was beset by the urge to tear it away, feel what lay hidden beneath.

"There's a hook here," he said, knowing full damn well Darla Cameron wasn't the type of woman who slept around. "Someone put you up to this, or you want something."

"I do want something," she said, her voice soft in the darkness. "Tonight I want you."

So there it was. Tonight was only a simple hookup. Outside, music played, and fireworks streaked across the sky, popping and hissing. If he opened the window to his second-story bedroom, they would see clouds streaking the moon on a cold Valentine's night. This would all be so romantic, if he wasn't suffering from the sixth sense that something wasn't right.

"How did you know I'd be sleeping in here and not the bunkhouse?"

"I know all the guests who are staying in the bunkhouse," she told him, moving his hand slightly so the sheet barely covered her breasts. He could feel heavenly softness just a brush away. Being this close to her at long last was killing him. Parts of him felt like the fireworks, ready to explode.

"And Fiona mentioned that you and some of your brothers were sleeping in the house so the guests could have privacy."

"So here you are."

"Here I am," she said, so sweetly breathless that he didn't have the heart to keep looking the gift horse in the mouth. Luckily, he had condoms in the nightstand, a groom's gift from Creed, who had a penchant for stupid gags. No silver letter opener for his groomsmen; no, just boxes of condoms with peace signs and neon inscriptions on the side. Creed's last laugh, since the brother with the most progeny won Rancho Diablo. Creed was the most competitive of the Callahans.

"All right," Judah said. "I've never thrown a woman out of my bed, and I certainly won't start now."

He didn't get why she was here, but he wasn't going to worry about it. Since the lady had hunted him down, he intended to make tonight very much worth her while.

TWO HOURS LATER, something made Judah start awake. After the hottest sex he'd ever experienced, he'd fallen asleep, holding Darla in his arms, grateful for the good fortune heaven had thrown his way.

Darla jumped from the bed. "I heard someone in the hall!"

"It's all right," he said, trying to tug her back for another helping of delicious blonde.

"It's not all right!"

She eluded his grasp, so he snapped on the lamp. She was tugging on her party dress like a woman fleeing a crime scene. "Hey," he said, "we're consenting adults. No one's going to bust in here and—"

"Shh!" She glanced at the door nervously. "I think the guests have all left. Your brothers will come upstairs any minute."

"And my aunt Fiona and Burke," Judah said, and Darla let out a squeak of fear.

"Get me out of here! Without anyone seeing me. Please!"

He'd prefer it if she stayed until dawn crested the New Mexico sky, but it was clear she was determined to pull a Cinderella and disappear. He got out of bed and pulled on his jeans.

"Can you zip me? Please?" She turned her back to him and Judah drank in all the smooth skin exposed to his hungry gaze.

"Are you sure you won't—"

"Judah, please!"

He zipped her, taking his sweet time as he pressed a kiss against her shoulder. "Even if any of my family were to see you, Darla, it's not like they'd brand you with a scarlet *A*."

"I shouldn't have done this. I don't know what came over me." She yanked on her heels, bringing her nearly four inches closer to his height. He reached for her, determined to show her how well suited they were, but she unlocked the door and dashed out before he could convince her to stay.

Shoving his shirt in his jeans, he hurried after her. He caught sight of a full blue skirt disappearing around the corner as she made it to the landing.

And then she was gone.

"Damn," Judah said. "I'm think I'm going to have to marry that girl."

Which was really funny, because of all his brothers, Judah had always known he would never marry. Not for his aunt, who dearly wanted to see all the Callahan boys married. Not for Rancho Diablo, which would go to the brother with the largest family. And not for love, because he really didn't believe in love. At least not with one woman.

But perhaps he'd espoused that view because he'd always secretly had a crush on the unattainable Darla Cameron. She'd never so much as glanced his way. She'd been a serious student in high school, gone on to be a serious student in college, gotten a grad degree and then become a serious nurse. No, she'd never really given any of the guys in town a look, so he'd figured his chances were slim. He couldn't even strike up a conversation with her.

All that changed tonight, he thought with a self-satisfied smile. And now that he'd had her, he was pretty certain he wouldn't be able to give her up.

FOUR MONTHS PASSED quickly when you weren't having fun, and Judah wasn't having any fun at all. Darla had barely spoken to him since that Valentine's Day evening. He'd tried to chat with her, done everything but go by the bridal salon and corner her, which his pride would not allow him to do. For a woman who'd seduced him, she'd certainly taken off fast. And lately, he'd heard she'd been lying low. Maybe wasn't feeling great. Aunt Fiona was no help to him, but had dared to nonchalantly ask after his Valentine's night surprise.

Obviously, Darla hadn't been as enthused about their lovemaking as he'd been.

The realization stung like gritty wind. This was worse than when he'd only worshipped Darla from afar. Now he knew what he was missing out on, and it made him hunger for her more. She was constantly on his mind. People said she wasn't taking phone calls, except from her mother, Mavis, who'd put out the word that Darla wasn't accepting visitors at her small bungalow.

He would bide his time. He *had* to have her. There was no other option. She was a treasure he alone was going to possess.

If he could just figure out how.

"The first annual Rancho Diablo Charity Matchmaking Ball was such a success, not to mention Creed and Aberdeen's wedding," Aunt Fiona announced to Judah as he slunk into the kitchen, "that I'm in the mood to plan another party."

He grimaced, not interested in discussing Fiona's die-hard love of partying. It was all an excuse for her to marry off her nephews. The trouble with having a committed matchmaker in the family was that it was embarrassing when said matchmaker couldn't fix his problem even if he wanted her to. He was sunk. "Do we really need another social function?"

"I think we do," Fiona said. "We raised a lot of money for the Diablo public library, and we made a lot of new friends. And we irritated the heck out of Bode Jenkins, which, as you know, is my life's goal. Not to mention you could stand a little perking up."

Judah grunted. "What do you have in mind?"

"Well," she said, moving around the sunny kitchen, "we need to find our next victim. The easiest way to do that is to keep ladies visiting the ranch." She sent him a questioning glance. "Unless you know something I don't know."

"Like what?" He settled in to eating the eggs and bacon she put in front of him. There were strawberry jam-smothered biscuits on the side, and a steaming cup of brew. Life was too good to mess up with another extravaganza. The feed bag was definitely better when Fiona's concentration was on the Callahans and not on impressing females far and wide. "I'm usually the last to know anything about anything."

"That's no surprise. What I meant was that unless you know that romance is blooming somewhere on the ranch—"

He shook his head, silencing that train of thought. "Dry wells around here, Aunt."

"Then let's choose a victim and get on with it. Time is running out."

He looked up reluctantly from his breakfast. "You got Pete and Creed married off. That's a third of us who've given up the flag of freedom. Maybe no more weddings are needed.

Or children," he added, knowing that was Fiona's real goal. "Pete has three, and Creed has Joy Patrice, but he brought three more with him if you count Diane's. Either way, that's a grand total of seven new kids on the ranch." He smiled, but it was pained. "Plenty, huh?"

She scowled. "Seven is hardly enough to make the case that our ranch shouldn't be sold for public land use. Bode'll never let us get off that easily. We need more."

Judah looked with sorrow at his eggs, his appetite leaving him. "Well, you could try Sam, but I think he likes the ladies a little too much to settle down with just one."

"And he's just a baby," Fiona said. "Twenty-six is too young when I've got hardened bachelors sitting around this place shirking their futures."

Judah rubbed at his chin. "Well, there's Jonas, but that would take too much work."

Fiona huffed. "You'd think a thirty-three-year-old surgeon would be a bit more anxious to find a wife, but *no-o-o.* I don't think he has the first clue about women, honestly. He's such a—"

"Nerd," Judah said, trying to be helpful, which earned him another scowl from Fiona.

"He's not a nerd. He's just a deep thinker."

That was an understatement. "You could pick on Rafe. He's next in line behind Jonas, and as Creed's twin it would make sense. He'll probably start missing that twin camaraderie now that Creed's got his hands full."

Fiona looked hurt. "Is that what you think I'm doing? Picking on you boys?"

"Oh, no. No, Aunt Fiona." Judah looked at the hurt tears in his delicate aunt's eyes. "We know you just want us all to be happy."

She nodded. "I do. And how do you think I feel about having to make you all settle down before your time—if you have a sense of time at all, and I don't think any of you boys do—when I've lost Rancho Diablo?"

"We haven't lost it yet," Judah soothed. "Sam's gotten a continuance. We may get out of Bode's trap eventually. Somehow."

"But it's better to load our deck for success." Fiona waved at him. "Eat your breakfast. It's getting cold."

Burke, Fiona's lifelong butler (and her secret husband, which she seemed keen for no one to know about, though all the Callahan brothers had figured it out) brought the mail in, handing it to her.

"Oh, look!" she exclaimed, as Judah pushed the now cool eggs around his plate. She waved an envelope in the air. "Cream-colored stock. Always a good sign!"

"Why?" he asked, his gaze on the calligraphed envelope.

"It's a wedding invitation, if I know my wedding invitations, and I think I do!" Fiona tore into the envelope. She stopped, staring at the contents. "Well," she murmured, "I didn't see this coming. No, I really didn't."

Burke looked over her shoulder, peering at the invite. "Uh-oh," he said, and Fiona nodded.

"Who's getting strung?" he asked, feeling cheerful that it wasn't him. Some other poor sack was getting the marital ball and chain, but it wasn't him. *Pity the fool who falls into the clutches of a beautiful woman,* he thought, as his aunt handed him the invitation silently.

"'Ms. Mavis Cameron Night requests the honor of your presence at the wedding of her daughter, Darla Cameron, to Dr. Sidney Tunstall, on June 30,'" he read out loud, his breath going short and his heart practically stopping. His gaze shot to Fiona's. "Didn't you know about this? She's one of your best friends."

"Mavis didn't say a word to me," his aunt exclaimed. "I

can't understand why. And the wedding is in a few days, which I also can't understand. What's the rush?"

She studied the invitation for another moment, then lifted her gaze to his again. Oh, but she needn't have worn such a worried expression. He had a good idea why a woman might marry so quickly—Darla was pregnant.

The thought burned his gut.

"Oh, dear," Aunt Fiona said, her eyes huge.

Judah shoved back his chair.

"Shall I say all the family will be in attendance?" she asked, and he yelled over his shoulder, "I wouldn't miss it," as he dashed out into the hot dry wind. Darla hadn't wanted any emotional connection between them. And he, spare Romeo that he was, had fallen into her arms and dreamed of a future.

He was a fool. But not a fool on his way to the altar, and there was something to be said for that.

Still, Judah wondered if he heard an empty echo in his bravado. And his broken heart drove him onto the range, riding hell-bent to nowhere.

AN HOUR LATER, Judah was positive he saw the mystical Diablos down in a canyon, well past the working oil derricks and the fenced cattle land. Legend said that the wild horses ran free on Rancho Diablo, and no one could get close to them because they were spirits. They were also a portent of something magical to come. The Callahans didn't see the herd of horses often, but when they did, they respected the moment.

They were not spirit horses, as far as Judah was concerned. He could see them drinking from a small stream that threaded through the dust-painted canyon, though his eyes blurred in the bright sunlight. Nearby, a large cactus offered a little shade, but Judah ignored it, easing back in the saddle to watch the horses. Their untamed beauty called to his own wild side.

They turned as one and floated deeper into the canyon.

Judah followed, watching for snakes, hawks and other critters. He and his brothers had explored this canyon many times, knew all its secrets.

His horse went to the thin stream, too. Judah slid from the saddle and took a long drink from the pale water. When he looked up, he saw a rock shelf he didn't remember.

Closer inspection showed the opening to a cave so hidden from the main canyon path that he would never have seen it if he hadn't bent down to drink. Cautiously, he went inside, his gun drawn in case of wild creatures he might startle.

But the cave was empty now—clearly some kind of once-used mine. Judah went past a rough shaft and a basic pulley and cart.

He'd found the legendary silver mine.

But it wasn't much of one, and appeared to have been long deserted. This couldn't be why Bode was so determined to get Rancho Diablo land—unless he thought there was more silver to be discovered. Still, what difference could silver mean to the wealthy man? And even if the Callahans were forced to sell Rancho Diablo, they would make certain they retained the mineral rights.

A loomed rug lay on the cave floor, hidden from casual visitors. There was also evidence of footprints, visible in the fading light that filtered into the cave. Still deeper, what seemed to be a message in some cryptic language was written on the wall, and it looked fresh. He touched the letters, smearing them a little. Underneath, silver coins and a few silver bars were stacked on a flat rock, like an offering.

Judah realized he'd stumbled on a smuggling operation, or perhaps a thruway for travelers who shouldn't be using Rancho Diablo land.

He left the cave, grabbed his horse's reins and swung into the saddle to ride in the opposite direction the Diablos had taken, as he wondered who might be using Callahan land and why.

For the moment, he would say nothing, he decided—until he understood more about why he'd been led to this place.

THE NEXT DAY, Judah realized drastic steps would have to be taken. The whole town of Diablo, it seemed, was atwitter over Darla's impending marriage. No detail was too small to be hashed over—the bridal gown she'd bought from the store she co-owned with Jackie Samuels Callahan, Pete's wife; the diamante-covered shoes she'd purchased. She'd scheduled an appointment for her hair, which had been dutifully reported. It would be worn long, crowned with an illusion veil that had orange blossoms cascading at the hem, which would just touch her shoulders.

Judah was sick to death of details. He wouldn't know an orange blossom if it grew out of his boot.

Strangely, the bride had not been seen since her invitations were mailed. Nor had the groom, though he was expected in town any day now. Judah knew him. Sidney Tunstall was a popular rodeo doctor and a one-time bronc buster, a man with a spine like a spring, who seemed to be kissed by good fortune. He was also wealthy. And he'd been after Darla for some time, if scuttlebutt was to be believed. Tall and lean and focused, the doctor seemed like a guy who loved what he did and did it well.

Which pretty much stank, but that was how it went. A man could lose to a better rival if he had slow-moving feet, and Judah reckoned his feet had been slower than most.

He flung himself inside the bunkhouse, anxious to sit alone in front of the fireplace to gather his thoughts.

It wasn't to be. Jonas was like a hulking rock in the den, taking up space with Sam and Rafe. And they'd been talking about him, Judah realized, by the way they shut their yaps the instant he entered.

"What's up?" he asked, eyeing them. "Don't stop talking about me just because I'm here."

"All right," Sam said. "Are you going to the wedding?"

The wedding. As if it was the only wedding in Diablo.

Actually, he hadn't heard of any other Diablo weddings lately, and if there'd been some, Fiona would definitely have been keeping the scoreboard updated for everyone, particularly him and his brothers. He sighed. "I might. Then again, I mightn't."

Jonas shrugged. "Let us know if you need anything."

"Yeah," Rafe said, "short of a shot of pride."

Judah blinked. "What's that supposed to mean?"

Sam gazed at him. "Look, bro. It's not like we haven't known forever that you've been carrying an inextinguishable torch for Darla Cameron. What we can't figure out is why you're letting her waltz off with another man."

"Maybe that's not how I see it," Judah said, "and maybe it's none of your business, anyway."

Jonas leaned back. "We could be wrong. Maybe you haven't always been in love with her."

"Darla and I are friends. That's it."

Sam sniffed. "As long as you're cool with it, we are, too. We support you, whatever you decide. I mean, if you get an itch to crawl through her bedroom window, we'll hold the ladder for you."

"No ladders will be necessary." Judah tried not to think about the few moments he'd held Darla in his arms. "She's chosen her man, and—"

"Ah-ha!" Rafe exclaimed. "You admit she didn't choose you!"

"She didn't choose any of you, either. It's not a special situation," Judah said, feeling cranky.

"So you admit you were in a position to be chosen," Sam said, sounding like the lawyer he was. "You were a candidate, if a slightly lazy one. But there's still time to present your case. Females change their minds like the wind. And ladies love it when a last-minute challenger shows up to yodel his heartstrings under ye olde bedroom window. I say go for it. Yodel away. You can borrow my guitar."

"Darla's doing just fine," Judah said. "Everything is in the works. She's got her shoes, her flowers and no doubt something blue."

"The really blue thing at that wedding is going to be you," Jonas said, "if you don't get up off your duff and speak before the forever-hold-your-peace."

There was no use. He was going to be harried to death by the people who should have supported his wish to be a silent sufferer. And this was light treatment, Judah realized, compared to what he'd probably be treated to in town, and especially at the wedding. Pitying looks, questioning gazes—

"What about the baby?" Sam asked. "What if it's yours?"

Judah frowned, aware of a sudden urge to stuff a fist in Sam's mouth. "What baby?"

Rafe studied him. "You know Darla is pregnant."

"Is that known?" Judah asked, his heart beating hard. "Or is it gossip based on her apparently whirlwind marriage?"

"She was seen buying a pregnancy test a while ago," Jonas said with a shrug. "This is a small town, and though she sent a friend in to purchase it, the bag made a clear exchange, which was duly noted by several people."

"Who were spying like old-time geezers," Judah said, not happy to hear confirmation of his own suspicions. "It doesn't mean she's pregnant. It could have been a negative test. She could have been giving it to Jackie, for all you know. And," he said, finishing with a flourish, "there's every possibility she's getting married because she wants to, and is in love, and the lure of owning her own bridal shop finally got to her. If you owned a machine shop, wouldn't it kill you if you could never use the tools?"

"Boy, are you caging your inner lion," Rafe said. "Hey, we've got your back, bro. We know how to shine the old badge of pride. No one will ever get from us how you got left in the dust." He shook his head, more sympathetic than Judah could stand.

"That's it," he said. "I've just seen a flash of my future, and I'm taking a rain check on it. The only way to get away from you bunch of know-it-alls is to disappear on you." Judah waved an expansive arm. "With no forwarding address. Don't even try to find me. Consider me gone with the wind, in order to save the dregs of my life." He crammed his hat on his head and turned to depart, with one last thought making him swing back around to his brothers, who watched him with open curiosity.

"And you can tell everybody in Diablo that my heart was not broken, thank you very much. You can tell them that rodeo was always my only love, and is to this day." He made a grandiose exit, proud of himself for the charade he'd perpetrated.

No one would ever know he was lying like a rug.

His brothers looked at each other after Judah left.

"Are we going to tell him that the boxes of condoms we all received at Creed's bachelor party were gag gifts? Creed's parting wish that we'd all get hung by our own family jewels?" Sam asked. "It's possible Judah didn't get the joke."

"I think we leave it alone," Jonas said. "Judah doesn't seem to want to consider that the child Darla might be carrying is his."

Rafe nodded. "*If* she is four months pregnant, as we hear she is, and the birth coincides with Creed and Aberdeen's wedding night, then it may be obvious."

"Why wouldn't Darla tell Judah?" Sam's forehead wrinkled. "That's the only thing that's not making sense. Wouldn't she just say, hey, that night of passion resulted in some passion fruit?"

"They've been running away from each other for so long, admitting that she's pregnant by Judah is the last thing Darla would do. He never acts as if he likes her, much less loves her. Ladies do not dig the strong, silent type when they need some reassurance, and Judah's been playing the role of Macho Man with gusto," Jonas said. "What woman wants a man if she thinks he doesn't love her?"

"Anyway, we're in way over our heads here," Rafe said. "We could have this all wrong. Maybe they never did the deed that night. Maybe Creed never saw them go off together. Darla could be pregnant by the bronc buster doctor, not that anyone ever mentioned them dating. It's not like we can ask her, because she's not even telling anyone she's in a family way. Rumors may be flying, but no one's going to mention them to the blushing bride."

They thought about the problem some more, then Jonas shrugged. "We'll know by November, I guess."

"Or not," Sam said. "She may choose to never reveal the real father."

"And Judah loses out on being a dad," Rafe mused. "Which would really be a loss, because he'd probably make a decent one. I mean, if Creed and Pete can do it, why not Judah?"

But there was nothing they could do about it. Darla was getting married, and Judah was gone, and neither one of them seemed to care that true love was being held captive by stubborn hearts.

"I hope I'm not that dumb when a beautiful woman loves me," Sam said with a sigh, and both his brothers immediately said, "You will be."

"But not as dumb as Judah," Sam muttered to himself, listening to Judah's truck roar away.

"I say it's time we engage Aunt Fiona," Jonas suggested, and his brothers nodded. "This situation could be dire."

"Maybe, maybe not," Sam said, "but Judah certainly isn't going to do anything to save himself."

Chapter Two

Rafe, Sam and Jonas went to the kitchen to find Fiona. As a rule, she or Burke could be found there, or nearby, at least. It was nearly the dinner hour, a very odd time for Judah to decide to depart, which just showed that even an empty stomach hadn't deterred his boneheadedness.

The kitchen was empty. The scents of wondrous culinary delights (Fiona could cook like no other, and Burke was no slouch in their shared gastronomic hobby) were absent. Rafe felt his stomach rumble and figured this might be an unannounced catch-as-catch-can night. They had those at Rancho Diablo, though rarely. Usually on the nights their fearless aunt had bingo or her book reading club or a church group, she cut them loose. But at least a pie would be left on the kitchen counter, with a note on the Today's Meal chalkboard that read something to the effect of "Tough Luck! You're Stuck!"

Tonight, all that was on the counter was a single bar of something silver. Rafe, Jonas and Sam crowded around it, perplexed.

"That's not cherry pie," Sam said.

"It's mined silver," Jonas said. "Mined and pressed into a bar. See the .925 on it?"

Rafe blinked. "Why would Fiona leave us a bar of silver?"

"All those years people have whispered about there being a

silver mine on our land suddenly comes to mind," Sam said, his voice hushed.

Rafe's gaze went back to the bar. "We've been over every inch of Rancho Diablo. There's no way."

"I don't know," Jonas said. "Why else would Aunt Fiona have a silver bar?"

"Because she's putting it in her stock portfolio," Sam said. "She bought some through a television advertisement, or a jeweler, to diversify her nest egg. It's not sound to leave all one's investments in the stock market or the national currency. She's just taken physical possession of some of her holdings, I would guess."

"But what if it's not part of her nest egg?" Rafe asked. "What if there really is a silver mine on Rancho Diablo? That would explain why Bode Jenkins is so hot to get this place."

They heard Burke whistling upstairs, and the chirping sound of Fiona's voice.

"Quick," Jonas said. "Outside."

They hustled out like furtive thieves. Rafe closed the door carefully behind him. His brothers had already skedaddled down the white graveled drive toward the barns.

Rafe hurried after them. "Why don't we ask her what it is? What if there is silver on the ranch? What if Bode is sniffing around for it?"

"Then she probably wouldn't have left proof of its existence lying out on the kitchen counter," Sam said. "By now, Bode's had this place satellite mapped, I'm sure. He's had the geographic and mineral composition of the land gone over. If there was silver around here, he would know before we would."

"All I'm suggesting," Rafe said, "is that maybe it's time we quit being so worried about offending Fiona. That we just ask her."

His brothers stopped, gave him a long eyeballing. Rafe

shrugged. "I mean, what the hell?" he asked. "If we have a silver mine, hurrah for us. It doesn't change anything."

"If there's a silver mine, and Fiona's been putting away dividends all these years, I don't want to know." Jonas shrugged. "Look, I love Fiona. I don't give a damn if there's solid gold under this ranch from corner to corner, and she plans to ferret all of it off like a conquistador. I really don't care. So I'm not asking."

Jonas had a point. Rafe didn't want to hurt Fiona's feelings, either. She'd given up a pretty decent life in Ireland to come take care of them, which couldn't have been easy. They had not been a snap to raise. "All right," Rafe said, "by now she's probably hidden the damn thing. So can we go back now, act like we didn't see it and go over the Judah problem with her? I'm pretty certain we need a guiding hand here."

They went back to the house, and this time, Jonas banged on the kitchen door.

Fiona flung it open. "For heaven's sake. Can't you open a door by yourselves? Three big strong men can't figure out how to use the key?" She glanced at the doorknob. "The door isn't locked. Why are you knocking, like this isn't your house?"

They stared at their tiny aunt. Her eyes were kind, her voice teasing, but she seemed truly mystified. Rafe swallowed. "Aunt Fiona, we wonder if you have a moment so we might pick your brain?"

"So you're standing on the porch? You won't pick it out there. When you're ready, come inside."

They went in, glancing at each other like errant school boys. "You bring up the joke condoms," Rafe said quietly to Jonas. "You're the oldest. I'm not comfortable talking about sex with my aunt."

Jonas straightened his shoulders. "It's not a conversation I want to have, but no doubt she's heard worse."

"That's true," Sam said. "You go for it, Jonas. We support you."

Fiona waved them into the kitchen, where they leaned against the counters. The silver bar was gone, which Rafe had expected. His brothers gave him the same "You see?" look, to which he simply shrugged. He was more worried about condoms than silver bars at the moment.

"Rafe wants to tell you something," Jonas said. "Right, Rafe?"

He gulped, straightened. "I guess so." He flashed Jonas an irate glare with his eyes. "Judah has departed."

Fiona nodded. "He said he longed to test his mettle on the back of an angry bull. I told him to have at it. Judah's been restless lately."

Rafe swallowed again. "Aunt Fiona," he said carefully, not sure how to begin, and then Sam said, "Oh, come on. It's not that hard."

Rafe gave his brother a heated look, wishing he could swing his boot against Sam's backside.

"Spit it out," Fiona said. "You're acting like you have something horrible to tell me. I've got butterflies jumping in my stomach just looking at you, like the time you came to tell me you'd burned down the schoolhouse. You hadn't, but you thought you had—"

Rafe cleared his throat. "Creed gave us all boxes of prank condoms at his bachelor party as a send-off."

Fiona looked at him. "Prank condoms?"

He nodded. "Different colors, different, uh, styles. In the box, there were 'trick' condoms. You were supposed to guess which of the twelve was the trick."

Fiona wrinkled her nose. "What ape thought of that?"

"Creed," Sam and Jonas said.

"I mean, the product." Fiona sighed. "Only an imbecile

would buy… Oh, never mind. None of you were dumb enough not to get the joke, so ha-ha."

"We hear rumors," Jonas said, trying to help his brother out, for which Rafe was relieved, "that Darla might be expecting a baby."

Fiona frowned. "What does that have to do with us?"

"Well, is she?" Sam asked.

"It seems there may be a reason for the marital haste." Fiona opened the refrigerator and took out a strawberry icebox pie. She cut them each a generous slice, and the brothers eagerly gathered around with grateful thanks. "I have a Books'n'Bingo Society meeting tonight, and I intend to ask my dear friend about this rumor."

"Creed thinks," Sam said, around a mouthful of pie, "that Darla and Judah may have had a…"

She glanced at him. "Romantic interlude?"

All three brothers nodded.

"Did you ask Judah?" she inquired.

They shook their heads.

She gazed at all of them. "Do we suspect joke condoms might come into play?"

"We fear they might have," Sam said. "They could have. I threw my Trojan horse away," he said hastily. "But then, I'm a lawyer. I read fine print. When a box says 'Gag gift only, not for use in preventing pregnancy,' I hurl it like a ticking bomb into the nearest trash can."

"Too bad," Fiona shot back. "I like babies, and four of you are dragging your feet."

"Worse than dragging our feet. Judah's gone away with a broken heart," Rafe said.

"And the joke may be on him?" Fiona eyed each of them. "You believe Darla's marrying this other man as a cover for a relationship she may have had with Judah?"

"What we're theorizing," Jonas said, "is that he may have

thought the condoms *were* the gag gift, not that they were useless." Jonas sighed. "I, too, threw Creed's gift in the trash. I didn't want hot-pink condom sex with anyone I know."

They all looked at him with raised brows.

"I threw mine away, too," Rafe admitted. "I'm afraid of children. At least I think I am. Or maybe I'm afraid of getting married," he said cheerfully. "When I watched Creed go down like a tranquilized bull, I said, 'Rafe, you are not your twin.'"

"It's possible Judah tossed them as well," Fiona said. "And for all we know, Darla isn't pregnant, although I wouldn't bank on it at this point." She wrapped up the strawberry pie and returned it to the fridge. "Rafe, run upstairs and look in Judah's nightstand, since that's where he stayed that night because of the wedding guest housing situation."

"Not me," Rafe said, "I never snoop."

Fiona elevated a brow. "We can't let him go all over several states rodeoing and maybe scattering his seed, so to speak. If he took the condoms with him, and if he honestly needs glasses so much that he can't read a box—"

"Who reads the label on a box of condoms besides Sam?" Rafe said. "You just whip the foil packet out and—"

"Go," Fiona said. "Your brother's future may be at stake."

"I'm not doing it," Rafe said, and he meant it.

Fiona plucked three straws from a broom. "Draw," she told the brothers. "Short straw plays detective."

A moment later, Rafe held the short straw. "It's not fair," he grumbled. "I'm the existential one in the family. I believe in reading, and thinking deep thoughts, not nosing into places I don't belong." But he went up the stairs. In his heart Rafe knew that Judah and Darla belonged together. But they couldn't just fall into each other's arms and make it easy on everybody. "Leaving me with the difficult tasks," he muttered, reluctantly opening his brother's nightstand.

And there was the black box of joke condoms with the hot-pink smiley faces, peace signs and lip prints.

"Hurry up!" Fiona bellowed from the stairs. "You're not panning for gold! The suspense is killing us."

Rafe grunted. He opened the box.

There were nine left.

"Uh-oh," he muttered, and went downstairs with his report.

"Three?" Fiona said, when Rafe revealed his findings. "Three have been…are missing?" She looked distressed. "I hope Judah hasn't had more than one situation where such an item might be called for."

They all looked at her, their faces questioning.

"One woman," Fiona clarified, and they all said, "Oh, yeah, yeah, right."

The brothers glanced at each other, worried.

Rafe shifted. "What do we do now?"

They all gazed expectantly at Fiona. This was the counsel they had come to hear.

She shrugged and put on her wrap. "Nothing you can do. No one can save a man if he decides to give up his ground to the enemy. Faint heart never won fair lady and all that. Good night, nephews," she said. "Wish me luck at bingo tonight!"

And she tootled out the door.

The brothers looked after her.

"That was not helpful," Sam said.

"I agree," Rafe said. "I thought she'd give us the typical, in-depth Fiona strategy."

"She's right," Jonas said. "And we should be taking notes to remember this unfortunate episode in our brother's life."

"We probably won't," Rafe said morosely, and sat down to finish his pie. "I heard once that men are slow learners." And he wasn't going to tell anyone that it was Judge Julie Jenkins, next-door ranch owner and Bode's daughter, who had thrown that pearl of wisdom at his head.

DARLA LOOKED AT Jackie Callahan, co-owner of the Magic Wedding Dress Shop. "Pull harder," she said. "I'm not letting out my dress. I just bought it."

Jackie tugged at the fabric. "The satin just doesn't want to give. And I don't think it's good for the baby...."

Darla looked at herself in the triple mirror. "I've been eating a lot of strawberries. I crave them."

"That shouldn't cause so much weight gain," Jackie said. "Not that you look like you've gained *so* very much."

"On ice cream," Darla said, aware that her friend was trying to be tactful. "Strawberries on top of vanilla ice cream."

"Oh." Jackie looked at her. "Maybe switch to frozen yogurt?"

"There's only a week before the wedding. I think the waistline isn't going backward on the measuring tape." She looked at herself, turning around slowly, and then frowned. "Something's not right."

"I think the dress is beautiful on you."

"Thank you," Darla murmured. "I'm not sure what's not quite right, but there's definitely something."

"Nerves?" Jackie said. "Brides get them. They want everything to be perfect. We've certainly seen our share of Nervous Nells in here."

"I'm not nervous," Darla said. *What I am is not in love. And that's what's wrong. I'm not in love with the man I'm marrying. And he's not in love with me.*

"Do you want to try a different gown?" Jackie asked, and Darla shook her head.

"No. This one will do." She went to change. The gown was not what was wrong. She could wear a paper bag, or a gown fit for a royal princess, and it wouldn't matter.

"Well," Jackie said as Darla came back out, "I think I know what the problem is."

She looked at her, hoping her dear friend, business partner and maid of honor didn't.

"You're not wearing the magic wedding dress," Jackie said. "You always said it was your dream gown." She smiled at Darla. "It worked for me."

Darla's gaze slid to the magic wedding dress. It was true. Ever since Sabrina McKinley had brought the gown to her, saying that it brought true luck to the wearer, she had known it was the only gown for her. It was the most beautiful, magical dress she'd ever seen. Sparkly and iridescent, it made her catch her breath.

But she couldn't wear it, not to marry someone she didn't love with all her heart. She was fond of her fiancé. Dr. Sidney Tunstall was a perfect match on paper. Even he'd said that. He needed a wife for his career, and she...well, she needed not to think about the fact that somehow she'd gotten pregnant by Judah Callahan even though she knew he'd conscientiously used a condom every time they'd made love that incredible night.

He would never believe this was his baby.

"I don't think I believe in magic," Darla said.

Jackie looked at her. "Magic is what we sell."

"I know," Darla said, "but these days, I'm concentrating on the practical." *Practical, not romantic. No magic, just the bare business proposal. And one day, I'll tell Judah the truth—after I've backed it up with a DNA test.*

She'd had hopes that he was in love with her—but she knew better. Hijacking a guy just because he'd spent one evening giving her the pleasure of her life was no way to win his heart. And especially not when he'd been so very careful with protection. Judah was definitely a hunk who didn't want to get caught. He'd always been the favorite of the ladies, and he never stayed with just one.

Practical. That was how it had to be.

JUDAH WAS INTO LIVING lucky. That was his new approach. He was going to swing by his tail in the jungle of life until he beat the jungle back. He was feeling mean and tough, and resolved to win. Focused.

He put his entry in for the rodeo in Los Rios, New Mexico, and smiled at the cute brunette who took his money.

"Haven't seen you in a while, Judah," she said. "Where have you been hiding?"

"On the ranch." He didn't want to think about Rancho Diablo right now. "But now I'm back, and I plan on winning. How many entries are there?"

"Nearly a hundred, all events totaled. You're just in time. We were about to close registration."

"Then I'm lucky," he said.

"You could get luckier," she said with a smile.

He took that in, maybe half tempted, then shrugged. "You're too good for me, darlin'," he said. He winked at her and headed off to find some drinking buddies, telling himself that he hadn't accepted the brunette's generous offer because he was in a dark mood—really dark. Refusing her hadn't anything to do with Darla Cameron.

But thinking about Darla reminded him that she was marrying another man, and he definitely didn't want to think darker thoughts than necessary, so he pushed her out of his mind. Broken hearts were a dime a dozen, so his wasn't special. He headed to the bar, glad to see some cowboys he knew.

He was welcomed up to the bar with loud greetings.

"You're in?" someone asked, and Judah nodded.

"I'm taking nine months on the circuit to see what I can do. If I can break even and stay healthy, maybe I'll stay until I'm old and gray." He took the beer that the bartender handed him, raising it to the crowd. "And one for all my friends."

His buddies cheered. Judah grinned. This was what he needed. A buddy chorus of men who understood life as he did.

The little brunette slid into the bar, sending a smile his way. Female companionship wouldn't kill him, either. He couldn't slobber in his beer over Darla forever.

He'd left his condoms at home.

And that was probably lucky, too. Judah sighed and looked at his already empty bottle. He didn't need to sleep with a female. He needed Darla, but Darla—damn her lovely just-right-for-him body—didn't need him at all. Just when he'd finally kissed the princess of his dreams—after forgoing the temptation for years—the princess had turned into a faithless frog.

Which just showed you that fairy tales had it all wrong. It wasn't the woman who always kissed the frog—sometimes it was the guy who got gigged.

Chapter Three

Darla wondered if she was making the right decision. Her whole world reeled as she left the doctor's office.

Twins. She was having twins. It was the last thing she'd expected to hear at her prenatal checkup. And now she knew why she was getting so big so fast, why her wedding gown was already tight. And her babies' father was the wildest of the Callahans.

Her phone rang, startling her. The display read Rancho Diablo. She didn't necessarily want to talk to Fiona at the moment, but a friendly voice was probably just what she needed. "Hello?"

"Darla, it's Sam Callahan. Get your jeans on, doll. We'll be by in five minutes to pick you up."

"Why?"

"We're getting up a convoy to go watch Judah ride. He needs all the hometown support he can get. He's in the finals, and we're borrowing Fiona's party van to take the cheering squad over to Los Rios. So get your boots on and put the cat out for the night."

She didn't have a cat, nor any reason to follow this Pied Piper. Nothing good could come of it. "Sam—"

"And we're picking up Jackie, Sabrina and Julie just for fun. You don't want to be the only girl left in town, do you?"

Put that way, no. But she was getting married in four days, and she was having twins. She was exhausted.

Then again, the last thing she wanted to do was sit around and think about how her life had spun out of control. And if everybody was going to the rodeo, what harm was there in going, too? "I'll bring my pom-poms."

"That's my girl," Sam said. "We'll take good care of you."

She hung up, feeling like a moth attracted to a bright, hot light. "All right, babies. We're going to go see Daddy ride a big piece of steak around an arena. Your first rodeo."

Her children might go to rodeos for years, and they would never know that strong, handsome Judah Callahan was their father. She shivered, thinking about that one wonderful night in his arms.

It would never happen again.

FIONA, RAFE AND JONAS waited as Sam hung up the phone.

"No woman wants to be left out of a party." Sam grinned. "Just like you said, Aunt Fiona."

She nodded. "Now remember, when two immovable objects are forced to move into the same space—"

"It's highly combustible," Rafe said. "Your play on physics is unique, Aunt."

She nodded again. "And remember step two…."

"I feel like a spy," Jonas said. "You'd better not ever play any of these tricks on me, redoubtable aunt."

"Oh, I wouldn't *think* of it," Fiona said, her eyes round.

Her nephews grunted in unison, not falling for that, and headed off to pick up the other ladies.

"Did you hear my oldest nephew, Burke, my love?"

"I did." He placed a gentle kiss against her temple. "I do believe he offered you a challenge."

Fiona smiled. "That's exactly what I heard, too. And I wouldn't dream of not accepting a challenge."

JUDAH WASN'T NERVOUS about his rides. He'd almost been carried by angel's wings on every one so far, so high did his bulls buck and thrash, so easily did he hit eight on every ride. Never in his life had he ridden so well. Somehow the bulls he'd drawn were rank, and somehow, he was unbeatable. If rodeo could always be so easy…and yet, in all his years of rodeoing, he'd never ridden like this. He was living in the moment, blessed by the rodeo-loving gods.

And then it happened. He was sitting outside, thinking about his next ride, pondering the bull he'd drawn—Lightfoot Bill was known for tricks, and better cowboys than him had come flying off—when the hometown crowd came whooping and hollering over to him. It wasn't a huge scene they made, just enough to let him know they'd brought practically every one of their friends, including Darla Cameron.

She was definitely pregnant. Even he, who had little experience with the changes of a woman's body, could see that the lady he loved was with child. Her tummy protruded despite the pretty blue dress she wore, and if his eyes didn't deceive him her breasts were taking on the shape of sweet cantaloupes.

Yum.

She was beautiful, Madonna-like. Judah's heart thundered as he met Darla's gaze.

His concentration went haywire. "Hello, Darla," he said, and she said, "Hi, Judah. Good luck."

And then she went inside the arena, and the other ladies kissed his cheek and wished him a long ride, and his brothers clapped him on the back with hearty thuds, telling him he was *the man!*

But he didn't feel like *the man.* What man wanted to see his ladylove pregnant by another guy? The thought cramped his gut.

He was a wimp. A romantic fool.

He dragged himself inside. A couple of his brothers rallied around, giving him a pep talk he didn't hear. "Why'd you bring her?" he asked dully.

"Who?" Rafe asked.

"Darla." He couldn't speak her name without feeling pain.

"We couldn't leave her behind," Sam said. "Now buck up, bro, and think about your ride. I heard Lightfoot took his last rider for a spin into the boards."

"Yeah." That rider had busted his leg and would be out for a few months. Judah put his mouth guard in, a preride ritual that always focused his mind on the next few moments.

His mind wouldn't cooperate. "She's beautiful," he said, and Sam said, "What?"

Judah couldn't form words clearly around the mouth guard and his rattled brain. It didn't matter. Darla wasn't his, wasn't ever going to be his, and that baby she was carrying was going to have a rodeo doctor for a daddy. Not him.

And then he realized why Darla was here. She hadn't come to see him. Her fiancé—husband-to-be in just a few days—was working the rodeo tonight.

"Well, I'm not going to need his services," he said, and Sam said, "What, ass? I can't hear you with that mouth guard in. Why'd you put it in if you were going to go all Oprah on me?"

Lightfoot Bill was in the chute. Judah got on the rails.

It was time to score big. All he needed was to keep riding like he'd been riding—and then it wouldn't matter that his heart was blown out.

Nothing was about to matter, except hanging on.

DARLA DIDN'T KNOW when she'd ever been so nervous. Jackie held her hand, and Sabrina McKinley clutched her fingers on the other side. "Having any visions?" Darla asked Sabrina.

"Only that you're having twins," Sabrina whispered back.

Darla looked at her in shock. "You really are psychic, aren't you?"

"I was teasing. Nice to know I can occasionally guess right." Sabrina smiled at her. "He'll be fine. At least I hope so."

Darla hoped the row of Callahan men behind them—and most especially Fiona—hadn't heard her big news. "Don't tell anyone. I'm still trying to get over the shock."

Sabrina laughed, and Jonas said, "What's so funny? My brother's about to ride down there." So the women shared an eye roll and went back to watching the arena.

The gate swung open and the bull came out jacked and on a mission. Darla was pretty certain her breath completely stopped. She didn't realize she was squeezing Jackie's and Sabrina's hands until the buzzer went off.

The brothers jumped to their feet, cheering for Judah. So did everyone else from Diablo. Darla sat back down, closing her eyes for a moment, awash in conflicting emotions. Judah scared her to death. He loved living dangerously. He always had. Her heart had always been drawn to that. She herself was practical, calculating risks and making sure she stayed in a safe zone.

She wasn't safe anymore. She was wildly in love with Judah Callahan, and in four days she was marrying someone who was not the father of her children. Her babies' father was down there being congratulated, so far away from her they might as well be in different hemispheres.

Judah's score shot him into second place, and Darla tried to breathe.

"Man, that was something!" Jonas said. "That bull laid out all the tricks it knew to get Judah off."

"He's got to be happy with that score," Rafe said. "Now, if he can just keep it going."

Darla closed her eyes, wishing she'd never agreed to come.

The nurse in her wished Judah had a safer calling; the practical side of her knew he was doing what he loved best.

Which was why she hadn't said a word to him about being a father.

"You'll have to tell him sooner or later," Sabrina said.

Darla stared at her. "Tell him what?" she asked, hoping her secret was still safe.

"That he's going to be a dad," her friend said.

"Hey, Sabrina," Fiona said from behind them. "I'm thinking about hiring you away from Bode. What would you say to that?"

They all turned to look at the older woman.

"Is that wise?" Sam asked. "Not that I don't approve, but won't that get Bode on you all over again?"

Fiona shrugged. "I'm in the mood to annoy Bode."

Burke said, "We could really use the extra help. There's been so many babies, and Fiona wants to spend all her time holding them."

Darla felt her heart drop again. Her children would never be part of the love in the Callahan household. It was their rightful place. There were a lot of people at Rancho Diablo who would love the twins, if they knew about them. And she had no right keeping Judah in the dark.

Suddenly, Darla knew Sabrina was right. She had to find a way to tell Judah—before she said "I do."

It wasn't going to be easy, and he probably wouldn't believe her. But her children deserved an honest start in life—no secret-baby surprises. Her gaze found Judah in the arena—though she should have been looking at her rodeo physician fiancé—and it seemed Judah glanced her way before he disappeared.

I'll tell him tonight.

IT WASN'T JUDAH'S POLICY to make love to a woman the night before a big ride. He had two more rides tomorrow. He was sitting on a big score tonight—second place was sitting pretty. It left him room to chase, but he wasn't the target. Second was great.

Therefore, lovemaking was the last thing on his mind.

Well, not the last thing. Every time he glanced up at Darla in the stands, looking like a hot dream, he had to fight his mind to focus.

He wasn't planning on making love.

But when she came to him and asked him if he had five minutes to talk to her—alone—a devil jumped to life inside him. "My room's across the street."

She stared at him, her cheeks pink. Oh, he knew her fiancé was here. He'd spoken to the good doc at least five times tonight. He didn't hold a grudge against the man.

If he held a grudge against anyone, Judah thought, it was this woman. She'd snared his heart, then trashed it. He didn't feel bad about reminding her that she'd once been behind a locked door with him.

"I can't go to your room." Darla's face was pale.

"Then talk here." He crossed his arms. "I'm listening."

"I can't talk to you here," she said, glancing around. "Isn't there someplace we can talk privately?"

Judah shrugged and turned back to taking off his gear. "My room."

She took a deep breath. "All right."

He was surprised that she relented. "Here's my key. I'll be there in five." He handed it to her, and she snatched it, looking around furtively, which almost made him smile. Darla did not do sneaky well. She was more sweet than sneaky. She must have something big on her mind if she was willing to rendezvous with him. Idly, he wondered about it, decided he'd never understand the mysteries of the female mind, and promptly dismissed it. She was probably going to do the guilt trip thing, like how the night they'd spent together hadn't meant anything, and now that she was getting married, if he would keep the little detail about their evening under his hat, she'd be eternally grateful, blah-blah-blah.

He'd act as if it hadn't meant a thing to him, either, and let her go on to her newly married life with a clear conscience.

But first he let her stew in her juices for a little bit. Then he followed after her, tapping on his door. She let him in.

"Well? What's so urgent?" He put *I'm a busy man* in his voice, so she'd get her soliloquy over with, thereby sparing both of them the agony.

Darla's eyes were huge as she stared at him; he could tell she was nervous. Judah kept his gaze away from her belly. Looking at her, knowing she was pregnant, was killing him. No man should be in love with a woman and know she was carrying another man's child.

"I'm pregnant."

"I can see that. Congratulations."

"Thank you." She swallowed. "Congratulations to you as well."

"Yeah. It was a lucky ride. I need a couple more tomorrow." He didn't look toward his bed, because if he did, he'd be tempted to drag Darla there. And he was a gentleman. Barely.

"I mean, congratulations to you, because you're having a baby, too."

He laughed. "Not me. I'm—" He stopped, looked at her carefully. Her face was drained of color. "You're not saying—"

She nodded. "I'm afraid so."

He stared at her, gazing deep into her eyes. Darla was not a dishonest woman. She wouldn't tell him this unless she believed it to be true. "I don't get it. How?"

"I don't know! Maybe there was a tear." She glared at him. "You'd know better than me."

He blinked. The condoms had been given to him by Creed at his bachelor party. The side of the box had read *For The Guy Who's Large and In Charge.* Judah remembered vaguely thinking all that might be true, and that it was pretty damn competitive of Creed to try to keep the other brothers from getting themselves in the family way, just so he could stay in the lead for the ranch.

Judah sank into a cracked vinyl chair near a tiny round table. "Why are you telling me this now?"

She breathed in deeply, obviously trying to calm herself. "I wasn't going to tell you at all. But then I realized that was wrong. I don't want to have secret babies."

"Babies?" His heart ground to a halt in his chest. *"Babies?"*

She nodded. "We're having twins."

Judah's world opened up, chasmlike. His pulse jumped, more fiercely than when he'd been on the back of Lightfoot. "You say we're—"

"Yes."

He passed a hand across his forehead, realized he was sweating under his hat. "I don't mean to be coarse, but how do you know that you're pregnant by me and not by your fiancé?" He wasn't about to say the man's name.

"Because I've never slept with him."

"Why not? Not to be indelicate—"

"It doesn't matter," Darla said. "We don't have that kind of relationship."

Maybe the man was an idiot. Maybe his thing didn't work. Judah couldn't believe that a guy who was fortunate enough to get a ring on Darla's finger wouldn't be making love to her like a madman every night. "Every man has *that* kind of relationship, darlin'."

She wore embarrassment like a heavy winter cloak. "When Sid asked me to marry him, we agreed on a business relationship. That's it, and no more."

Sid. Judah leaned back, trying to take in everything he was hearing. "That's why you were so eager to get in my bed that night. You wanted a good time before you tied yourself to this *business* relationship."

She hadn't been interested in business with Judah.

A blush crossed her cheeks. "I—yes. And I'm not sorry about it. Even now."

"Nice to know you don't regret it." He couldn't help the sour tone in his voice. "So what does Tunstall think about you being pregnant?"

Darla stared him down. "It was unexpected, obviously, but he's not opposed to being a father."

Judah jumped to his feet, crossing to her. "Let me tell you something, Darla Cameron. If you're telling the truth—and something tells me you are—no one will be a father to my children but me. Let's just get that straight up front." He studied her, deciding it was time this relationship got on the right track. "Something's going to have to change about your wedding plans, sweetheart."

Darla shook her head at him. Judah was angry. She'd expected anger, but not his statement about her wedding. "What exactly does that mean?"

He went back to his chair, dropping into it with an enigmatic smile shadowing his lips. "It means you've got the tiger by the tail, and now you're going to have to tame it. I shouldn't have to spell anything out for you. You knew when you told me this that your wedding to the good doc was never going to happen."

"I know no such thing!"

"You're not marrying another man while you're carrying my children. So put all that out of your sweet head."

Darla felt her own stubbornness rise. "I'm not having children out of wedlock when I've got a perfectly good groom planning to be my husband, Judah. It's no inconvenience to you if I'm married. You're not planning on being around."

She could see by Judah's expression that he was fighting to be civil. But he didn't have the right to tell her how to run her life.

"It'll be inconvenient for you when two grooms are standing at the altar with you on your wedding day," Judah said.

"You're not suggesting that you want to marry me?"

He nodded. "If you're pregnant by me, the only man you're marrying is me. That's the way *I* do business, babe."

Annoyance rose inside her. "Not that I expect romance in a proposal, but I don't want to be told what I'm going to do, either."

"And I don't want to be told that I'm going to be a father, and that someone else is planning to raise my children." He gave her a determined stare. "I'm being very reasonable, under the circumstances."

This was awful. No woman wanted the man she loved this way. Darla wished she could walk out the door and forget these past ten minutes had ever happened. But she couldn't. Her pride couldn't be the most important thing to her right now—she had her children's welfare to consider. "I'll think about your proposal," she said coolly, going to the door.

"You do that, and don't forget to tell the good doc your business merger's off." Judah followed, putting his hand on the doorknob to open the door for her—at least that's what she thought he was going to do—before pressing his lips against her cheek, his stubble grazing her skin ever so slightly. "Just so you know, Darla, I don't plan on mixing business with my marriage."

His meaning was unmistakable. His hand moved to her waist in a possessive motion, lingering at her hip just for a second, capturing her. She remembered everything—how good he'd made her feel, how magical the night in his arms had been—and wished his proposal was made from love and not possessiveness.

Judah pulled the door open. "Next time I see you will be at the altar. Till death do us part, darlin'."

Darla stared at him for a long, wary second before stalking off.

If Judah Callahan thought she was going to marry a hard-headed, mule-stubborn man like him, then he was in for a shock.

Chapter Four

Judah had never been one to let someone else fight his battles. So it wasn't even a stretch for him to hunt up Dr. Sidney Tunstall. The good doctor was taking a breather in a bar down the street, which was good because Judah needed a drink himself.

First things first. "Tunstall," he said, seating himself next to the ex-bronc buster. "We have business to discuss."

Sidney put down his beer and gave him a long look. "Do we?"

Judah nodded. "I think it's only fair to let you know that you'll be hearing from Darla that your wedding is off."

The doctor raised a brow. "And how would you know?"

"Because," Judah said, "we just finished having a chat, Darla and I. And we came to the same conclusion. She can't marry you."

Sidney finished his beer, waved for another. "I'll wait to hear that from her, if you don't mind, Callahan."

"See, though, I *do* mind." He put down the money to pay for the beer. Sidney grunted, not about to utter any gratitude, and Judah couldn't blame him. "Darla says she's expecting my children. So that means she'll be taking the Callahan name. *My* name."

Sidney turned. "I happen to know that Darla thinks you're an ass she wishes she'd never met. And she's never mentioned you being the father of her children, so as far as I'm concerned, you're not even in the picture." He raised his bottle in a sardonic wave. "Thanks for the brew, but buzz off and let me drink it in peace."

Judah elected to ignore the insult. "What do you mean, you don't know about her being pregnant by me?"

The doctor shrugged. "We never talked about it. I don't need to know everything in her past. And until I know better, you *are* her past."

Judah slumped on his bar stool for a moment. He couldn't be mad at Tunstall—the man clearly wasn't in possession of all the facts. Just like a woman to leave out important details. Judah stood, tossed some tip money on the bar. "Look, Tunstall, you're an innocent party here, so I'm going to cut you some slack. But don't get in my way. I'll be standing at the altar with Darla, I'll be raising my own sons, and that's just the way it is."

"Maybe," Sidney said, "and maybe not."

The man had no idea how thin Judah's temper was at the moment. It was all he could do not to pound good sense into him. But Darla was the person he needed to be setting straight, so he took a deep breath and sauntered off to collect his wits before his rides tomorrow.

It wasn't going to be easy. His concentration had never been so scattered.

He couldn't decide if it was suddenly finding himself altar-bound or becoming a father that had him the most bent.

"HOW *DARE* YOU?" Darla demanded when Judah made it to his motel room an hour later, where she was waiting outside the door. He cast an appreciative eye over the snapping fire in her blue eyes, and her long blond hair. She looked like an angel, but she was going to bless him out like a she-devil.

Which meant that Tunstall had given her the bad news. And that suited Judah just fine.

"I dare," he said, unlocking his door and stepping inside his room with her on his heels, "because that's what I do. *I dare.*"

Her lips compressed for a moment. "You have no right to interfere."

He tossed his hat into the chair. "Just one man chatting with another. Don't get your panties in a twist over it, sugar." Grinning, he pulled a beer from the six-pack his brothers had thoughtfully left in his room, satisfied that matters should be straight as an arrow between him and his buttercup.

"I'm not going to marry you, Judah." Darla's chin rose, and her tiny nose nearly pointed at his chin. He so badly wanted to run his finger down her face and tell her everything was going to be just fine, if she'd only settle down and let him take care of her.

"We'll talk about it tomorrow after I ride. There's a lot of things we'll have to plan, like naming my sons. You'll need to enroll in a prenatal yoga class, too. I hear it's very beneficial for the mother and the babies."

Darla's cheeks went pink. "I'm leaving now," she told him, "and I *am* marrying Sidney. Quit trying to take over my life."

"Whew," Judah said, pulling her close against his chest. "You'll know when I'm trying to take over your life, babe. I'll say, 'Get in my bed,' and you'll go happily because you'll know I'm going to make you feel like a princess."

Irate as Darla was, she leaned into him, and for a moment, completely relaxed.

But she suddenly pulled herself away and marched to the door. "Not a chance, Judah. Goodbye."

THE NEXT DAY Darla carried the magic wedding dress to the back of the store where she couldn't see it. Lately, it had begun to call to her with a siren song of such temptation that she could barely resist it.

"Just try on the gown," Jackie urged. But Darla didn't want to fashion hopes and dreams through simple fabric.

"I don't need fairy tales and magic in my life. I'm making a solid, practical decision to marry a man who's as even-keeled as I am. Judah is a winter wind blowing through a canyon. I could never rely on him."

"But he's the father of your children," Jackie said. "You don't want to do something in the heat of passion, Darla."

"I already did that," she replied, "which is why I'm choosing to be quite selective with my children's futures now. Sidney will be a good father. He comes from a very small family, and has always wanted a large one. We're good friends. I'll be an organized, supportive doctor's wife." Darla stowed the magic wedding gown in the very back of the stock closet, behind back-stock dresses. It did lure her. Sometimes in the night, she could hear a faint rustle of musical chimes, like an antique jewelry box opening to play a lilting melody. The dress was beautiful.

And she wanted it so badly. But she wouldn't admit that to Jackie. Darla wanted to believe in romance and dreams and fairy tales, just like any other bride. Yet she couldn't afford any mistakes. Her whole makeup was geared toward thoughtful, careful decision making. There really wasn't any room for loving a bonehead like Judah.

Unfortunately for her, that bonehead made her body shiver and ache every time she thought of him. It was like that wild winter wind blew over her skin, reminding her of how much she loved him.

But that was the problem. She did love Judah—and she was just another responsibility for him, much like the ranch, and his family, and rodeo. Nothing special or different. Something he had to rule over, boss, command. Before their night together, he'd never spoken to her, nothing more than a passing hello and chitchat about the weather. And he hadn't so much as sought her out at the store since that night, either.

A woman knew when she was the object of a man's passions, and she wasn't that to Judah. He was too wild for her, too unsettled for a woman who liked calm rational choices in her life. Judah was her one moment of reckless abandon—and it didn't take a psychic gift to know they were not meant to be.

"Speaking of psychic," Darla said, and Jackie glanced up.

"Were we?" she asked.

"No, but is Sabrina really going to work for Fiona?"

"I think so. Why?"

"Because I was thinking about asking her if she wanted to work in the shop while I'm out after the babies are born. You can't do it all by yourself," Darla said, staying in practical mode.

"I'll be fine," Jackie assured her.

"You have three little ones. We need backup."

The door swung open, sending the bells over the shop door tinkling. Judah strolled in, the man of her dreams obviously on a mission, judging by the hot gleam in his eyes. Darla's heart jumped into overdrive.

"We need to talk," he stated, and Jackie said, "I'll be heading out for a coffee break. Nice ride last night, Judah."

He tipped his hat to her, and when the door swung shut behind her, he put the closed sign in the window.

"You can't close my shop," Darla said.

"We have to talk."

"Not while I'm working."

"The brides of Diablo will just have to wait while you take a fruit and juice break." He handed her a small bag. "Organic. Every bite."

She began to seethe. "I eat healthy, Judah. You don't need to concern yourself with my diet."

He nodded. "A husband takes care of his wife."

"Not to point out the obvious—"

He handed her a box. "Darla, you have to quit being so stubborn."

"What's this?" She eyed the small dark box as if it were a bomb.

"What a man gives a woman he wants to marry." He grinned, clearly pleased with himself.

She handed it back. "I'll keep the organic breakfast. You can keep your Pandora's box."

He put it on the counter. "If you don't want me to romance you, I'll stop."

"Thank you." She folded her arms.

He shrugged. "If that's the way you want it."

She didn't say anything to confirm his statement because it really wasn't the way she wanted it. But under the circumstances, "no" was the only option. Judah was a conqueror. He wanted to bulldoze her ivory tower and take her prisoner—but letting him do so would be a mistake.

"Why aren't you at the rodeo?"

"I can't ride when I'm all torn up like this."

That stopped her. She checked his eyes for signs of amusement, found none. Surely he was jesting, though. Judah wasn't a man whose emotions ruled his life. He was all action, sometimes even brave, fearless action. She again checked his expression for teasing, but he looked just as deadly serious as he had a moment ago. It was like gazing into the eyes of an Old West gunslinger in a classic movie: resolute, determined, honest.

She caught her breath. "We don't know each other at all."

He looked at her. "We know each other well enough to be parents."

"It's not enough, Judah. Marriage between two people who don't love each other is a mistake."

"So marrying Sidney would be just as big a mistake," he pointed out.

She took a step back. "I meant that marrying you when you never loved me would be a mistake. And you can't say that you do, Judah."

He remained silent, and she felt he'd conceded her point.

"If you're worried about having access to the children, you'll always have that."

"That can be taken care of legally," Judah growled. "I don't waste any energy worrying about that."

She blinked. "Legally?"

"Sure." He shrugged. "I could have Sam draw up custodial papers tonight if I was worried about you keeping me from my children. That's the least of my concerns."

"It's very nice to know that you've considered all your options, even as you bring me a token of your questionable affection."

His lips thinned. "That's not what I meant."

She turned away. "It doesn't matter, Judah. I don't want to marry you."

"Guess I'll have to take the good doc out and ask him what his secret is."

She whirled around to face him. "There isn't a secret. We have a lot in common. I like the security of knowing that I'm marrying someone a lot like me."

"Sounds boring." Judah leaned against the counter, giving her a lazy smile. "You're too sexy to be boring."

"Sexy?" She looked at him, startled.

"I think so." He shrugged. "Does Sidney?"

"I don't...I don't know," Darla said, confused. "I don't believe so. I mean, why would he?"

Judah grinned at her, and suddenly Darla felt like a mouse in the paws of a playful lion.

"I don't know why he wouldn't," Judah said. "Maybe you

should ask ol' Sid." He pushed himself away from the counter, approaching her too quickly for her to step away, even if she'd wanted to, which she didn't. Not really. She was kind of curious to see what new trick he had up his sleeve.

And she wanted him to kiss her. Just once more, to see if it was as good as she remembered.

He stopped in front of her, towering like a strong redwood tree. "I'm sure almost anyone would say that the good doctor is the better man. I know you'll rest comfortably with your very prudent decision."

"Quit being a rat," Darla snapped, and Judah kissed her—on the forehead.

The jerk. She wanted his lips on hers, and she had a feeling he knew it.

"I know when I'm beat." Judah strode to the door, tipped his hat, then placed it over his heart. "Congratulations. And I'll let ol' Sidney know that I have stood aside, his bride having made her choice."

Darla stared as he flipped the closed sign to Open, and loped down the main street of Diablo. Judah Callahan was the most maddening man she'd ever met. Why she'd ever slept with him, she didn't know.

Passion. She'd wanted one night of passion, which she knew Judah would give her, before she did the practical thing and married Dr. Sidney Tunstall. She'd wanted a lusty bedding before her marriage of convenience shut her up in a gilded prison of diligent routine for the rest of her life.

"I have no regrets," she murmured, and then her gaze fell on the small jeweler's box Judah had left on the wrap stand, next to the healthy snack he'd brought her.

She glanced once at the door to make certain he wasn't outside spying in on her, ready to tease her if she gave in to temptation. But Judah was long gone. There was a crowd on the sidewalk, so she knew that several women had run to chat with him, Judah being a female magnet like all the Callahan men.

Darla's hand rested on the jeweler's box.

Chapter Five

It was one of those days, Judah thought, as he picked himself off the ground. Some days you were the hero, and some days you were the dust between the hero's toes.

Today he might have been the dust under a very ordinary man's feet. Crazy Eight had thrown him within three seconds. It hadn't even been a decent ride. Crazy Eight hadn't been anything spectacular. But just as he'd left the chute, Judah had seen Sidney Tunstall out of the corner of his eye, and somehow his concentration had gone to hell.

He'd gotten thrown so easily a child could have ridden better. Judah slowly wandered over to the rail, slapping his hat against his leg. And somehow, he didn't seem to care. He wondered if Darla had opened the box with his offering in it. A man had to be prepared to fight like a soldier, and Dr. Tunstall was nice enough, but Judah understood women. And what he understood best about women was that a big sparkly diamond sometimes won the fair maiden.

Dr. Tunstall hadn't ponied up yet, so Judah had no compulsion about trying to get the jump on the competition. He'd called Harry Winston's and given a description of exactly what he wanted, then flown to pick it up. And it was a sparkler, like a star plucked from the sky.

No woman could resist it.

"And you know," he said to Sidney when the doc came over to check him out, "I went for the biggest star I could find."

Sidney looked at him. "How do you feel, Judah?"

"Like a winner," he said. "How do you feel, Doc?"

Sidney grunted. "Let's get you where I can take a look at you." He slipped an arm under Judah's, and helped him to a seat.

Then he passed one finger in front of Judah's face. "How many?"

"How many what?" Judah asked.

"Fingers?"

Judah sighed. "I see five fingers, which are going to be a knuckle sandwich, Doc, if you don't get your bony hand out of my face."

Sam came over to stare into his eyes. "Hey, bro. Hearing little birdies or anything? Faraway music? Fairy whisperings?"

Judah drew in another deep breath. "I don't have a concussion. I wasn't paying attention and I got thrown. That's all."

Rafe bent to stare into his face. "That was a doozy of a toss you took. Hit your head or anything?"

It was impossible to convince anybody that his problem wasn't in his head. His problem was in his heart. "If everyone will get out of here, I'm going to get ready for my next ride."

"Assuming I approve you to ride," Sidney said, and Judah glared at him.

"If you don't pass me to ride, I'll kick your ass."

Sidney nodded. "Unprovoked aggression. Loss of concentration. Could be a concussion."

Judah narrowed his eyes. "Don't pull that doctor mumbo jumbo on me. If you keep me from riding, it'll only be because you're trying to keep me from winning. You don't want me to win because you know ladies love cowboys who do. And I am in a serious position to be loved."

Dr. Tunstall shook his head. "I should let you ride. It would serve you right if I let you land on your already cracked head. Maybe it would knock some of the hot air out of you and serve to flatten that outsize ego of yours. But as it is," Dr. Tunstall said, "you're going to have to scratch."

"I will not scratch," Judah declared, and Sidney said, "Then I'll scratch you myself. Either way, your rodeoing is over for the next month."

"Month!" Judah hopped to his feet, heading after the departing doctor. "You can't keep me out for a month. I need to ride to make up the points for the finals. You know that as well as anyone."

"I do." Sidney glanced at him before he went back out to the arena to observe the next riders. "Go home and rest, Judah. Don't do any handsprings or jump off any houses, and you should be fine in a few weeks."

"I don't remember hitting my head," Judah muttered, glaring after him. "He's trying to keep me out of the rodeo."

"Well, that's a shame," Sam said. "Now you'll just have too much time on your hands to hang around Diablo and convince Darla that you'd make a better husband than a cowboy."

Light dawned. "Yeah," he said, "that's what I'll do. I'll cede this hallowed ground and grab territory closer to where yonder princess lays her fair head."

"Oh, jeez," Sam said. "Let's get you to the E.R., bro. I think you've stripped a gear."

DARLA HAD BEGUN TO OPEN the box Judah left, but then, not wanting to know what she was passing up, she'd snapped it closed without getting past the first crack in the hinge.

There was no point in torturing herself, since she wasn't marrying him. Ever. He wasn't above tempting her, but she would not succumb. Especially not since she had a wedding in a couple days.

The very thought made her break out in nervous hiccups, something she hadn't done in years. Jackie had gone home, the store was closed for the night and Darla was alone with her thoughts, and a hundred wedding gowns mocking her. She hiccupped twice in rapid succession. The magic wedding gown secreted in the storeroom called to her, dragging her thoughts to it. Temptation—wondering how she would look in the gown of her dreams—tugged at her.

She hiccupped again, painfully and loudly, in the silent store.

She had to know. It would wipe the last questions from her mind, and she could go on with her marriage to Sidney, knowing that a gown was just a gown, after all. It was the groom who made the day special for a bride, a man a woman knew she could trust to be at her side and…

And what? Take care of her? She didn't need that.

But Sidney would expect to take care of her. Judah wouldn't, she mused. He would expect to make love to her most days of the week, and be the guiding light in her life.

Sidney would not expect such hero worship.

Why she was even thinking about both men, comparing them, was a mystery. One of them was about to become her husband. The other wasn't going to be anything more to her than he'd ever been, just a casual acquaintance—with whom she now shared future parenting.

"Argh!" Darla hiccupped wildly. Dashing into the stockroom, she tore the magic wedding dress off its hangar and slipped it on, entranced by the luscious whisper it made sliding over her skin. The dress seemed to enfold her in its beauty, pouring dreams into her heart. The hiccups ceased; her nerves unfurled.

Taking a deep breath, she stepped to the mirrors.

The gown was simply stunning, glinting and sparkling with sequins and crystals, and a luminescence all its own emanating from the fabric. Darla's breath caught as she looked at herself, turning slowly to see all views in the mirrors. It was everything Sabrina had claimed. The same spell that had captured Jackie was now shimmering around her, gentle motes of magic that made her feel like a real bride.

Slowly, Darla gave in and opened the jeweler's box, gasping at the lovely diamond ring. Never had she seen a ring so utterly perfect. Unable to resist, she slipped it on her finger. It fitted perfectly, as if made to order.

Her gaze bounced to the mirrors and caught. She stared, astonished to see herself transformed into a fairy-tale bride.

And behind her, smiling a sexy *you're-all-mine* smile, was her handsome prince.

DARLA WHIRLED AROUND. He wasn't here. Her prince was a figment of her imagination—fantasy, wishful thinking, whatever. She hurried to take off the ring, shut it back in its box. She'd had no business trying it on.

And then she felt it, like a butterfly wing brushing against her neck: his lips, pressing against her fevered skin. Darla glanced into the mirror with longing as she watched Judah's ebony head dip to the cradle of her shoulder.

Before she could totally lose herself in the fantasy, she tore the magic wedding dress off and rapidly dressed, fingers shaking as she put on her own clothes. It was unsettling how much time Judah spent in her thoughts. He practically *lived* there, teasing her subconscious.

"It can't go on like this, buddy," she muttered, slipping on her shoes. "Once I'm married to Sidney, you are banished to the bin of ex-boyfriends."

Ex-lover, to be exact, but she'd fudge a little, one day in the future, when her children asked her about their real father. She'd say Judah Callahan had been a boyfriend, someone she'd cared about, but that they just hadn't loved each other....

Except she did love Judah. Darla swallowed against a tight throat and quickly turned off the store lights, locked the door, ran to her vehicle. Of course she loved him. She'd had a crush on him forever. Once they'd made love, she was lost to him.

And, she thought fiercely, *I'm glad I'm having his babies. It's a piece of him I never dreamed I'd have.*

"KEEPING IN MIND THAT you've always been a bit irascible," Fiona said, "Judah, this is irritable, even for you."

He sighed, taking the piece of triple chocolate fudge cake she'd brought him. He was going to get fat if Fiona didn't stop ministering to him. Once he'd scratched from the rodeo—very much against his will—and come home, his aunt had appointed herself his watchful angel. He was in bed reading at eight o'clock at night only because he didn't want to hang out with his brothers, who were playing, of all stupid things, badminton under the lights with their wives.

Judah munched dutifully on the delicious cake. "Aunt, you're going to make me fat. I'm not supposed to ride, I can't even play hopscotch with the kids for exercise. Every time I open my eyes, you're stuffing my face with some delicacy." He waved his fork. "You don't have to feed me. I'm capable of making a run to the kitchen myself."

"I'm sure you are." Fiona seated herself on the foot of his bed with a little bounce. "Are you certain you're comfy? Pillow soft enough for your aching head?"

Sighing, he put the cake on his nightstand and sat up, already wishing he had a handful of aspirin. Or an aunt-chaser, like a double whiskey. "What's this all about?"

"Judah," she said, her gaze pinned on his, "I know you found the cave. And I need for you to keep its existence under your hat."

He blinked. "How'd you know I found it?"

"I found your big boot prints there. And Burke had seen

you riding that way. Promise me that you won't breathe a word about it. To anyone. Not even…not even Darla."

Judah studied the determined gleam in his aunt's eyes. She was really worked up about this, hence the angelic caregiving she'd been heaping on him. He should have remembered she liked to bake when she was worried about something. "I haven't mentioned it to anybody. I've been preoccupied, and I also needed time to think about why it might be there. But I'd like to know why you're keeping it a secret. Is it because of Bode?"

"Partially," Fiona said, "and partly because we use it often."

"So is that the silver mine everybody's asked about over the years?" Judah reflected on that for a moment. "At one time or another, I guess just about the whole town has gossiped about it. Do we own a silver mine?"

"Not exactly," Fiona said carefully. "You might consider that cave a gift from a friend."

"What friend?"

She glanced at her hands. "I need to know that I have your absolute confidence."

He took another bite of cake, transfixed by his aunt's caginess. It was almost like when she'd told them childhood bedtime stories. She was spinning a great one right now—he could practically hear her thoughts churning. "I wouldn't breathe a word of this to my closest brother."

She sniffed. "Since you have five of those, I guess that's plural."

"Absolutely." He waved his fork again imperiously. "Speak on, aunt of many tales."

She gave him a sharp look. "This is not a fairy tale. More than you can realize hangs on the complete secrecy of that cave."

"I know, I know. But you shouldn't be crawling around in that place," Judah said. "It makes me nervous to think about you being there. What if you stumbled onto a snake? What if a coyote was in there? We never knew you had a secret hangout."

"Nothing will happen to me. Burke usually goes with me."

"Oh, so Burke is in on this as well," Judah said, growing more fascinated by the moment. "Do the two of you make midnight runs out there to dig up silver?"

She sighed. "I'm going to pop that concussed head of yours if you don't pay attention."

"Go. I'm all ears." He set down the plate and swigged the milk she'd set on his nightstand. The copy of *Death Comes to the Archbishop* he'd been reading fell to the floor, but he didn't notice.

"I have a friend who comes once a year to visit," Fiona began, and Judah said, "The Chief."

She nodded. "The silver is his. The cave is his home, of sorts."

"Is there a tribe around here?"

She nodded again. "But he sometimes stays in the cave. Alone. We won't ever tell anyone that."

"Is he a fugitive? Illegal?" Judah arranged a stern look on his face. "Aunt, we shouldn't be harboring someone who has some kind of record—"

She shook her head. "The cave is his. Your parents bought Rancho Diablo land from him—from the tribe, actually. The cave and the mine stay in his hands, all of those mineral rights being signed over to him."

"Why?"

"It was a fair exchange," Fiona said simply. "Your father negotiated for the land with the stipulation that the mine remained in the tribe's possession. It will be this way for always." She took a deep breath. "And one more reason why I absolutely must keep this ranch from falling into Bode's clutches."

"Oh." Judah had the whole picture now. "So Bode really wants the mine?"

"He wants everything. The mine, which he's only heard rumors about, but which he suspects must be real. The two working oil derricks, the land, the Diablos. He wants it all."

"No one can own the Diablos. They're free."

"For now," Fiona said. "As long as they are on Callahan land, the spirits are free."

A cool breeze passed over his skin. "And if we lose the ranch?"

"Everything is lost. The mine, and the secret that the mine hides."

"Surely there's not all that much silver. It was a small cave, as caves go."

Fiona looked at him sharply, her mouth opening as if to say something. Then she closed it, before rising to put his book on the nightstand and collecting his dishes. "Try to rest. I believe the doctor said a concussion requires absolute stillness for forty-eight hours, in your case."

"Funny thing is, I don't remember hitting my head," he complained. "I swear it's a conspiracy to keep me from riding."

"You'll live to ride another day if you rest now," Fiona said with a smile. "Good night, nephew."

"Good night, Aunt. Thanks for telling me about the cave. I'll take the secret with me to my grave."

She looked at him, her eyes deep and troubled. "You have no idea how much is riding on your ability to do just that." Then she left his room.

Judah felt restless now that he'd heard so much family lore. Inaction was never his strong suit.

What he needed was someone to annoy, to take his mind off all the family stuff. Nothing like a little late-night foray to make a man feel less starved for adventure.

Instead of staying here and allowing Fiona to put ten pounds on him, he decided to go make a different kind of midnight raid. After hearing about Bode bothering his aunt and the family treasure, he was in a dangerous mood.

JUDAH HESITATED ONLY ONCE, and that was in the hall outside Jonas's old room, where Sabrina now resided. Normally, the brothers slept in one of the large bunkhouses, having moved out once they hit the teen years, though occasionally they slunk back to their old rooms in the main house if they had an injury, which, thankfully, wasn't often. But it was easier to be where Fiona wouldn't have to run out to check on them twenty times a day, which she did when they were injured, no matter how many times they told her it wasn't necessary. His brothers hadn't even asked him where he wanted to sleep off his trifling—in his opinion—concussion; they'd dumped him unceremoniously at the house.

But Jonas shouldn't be in residence, nor any of the other brothers. Judah froze outside Sabrina's room, surprised by the answering murmur of a man's voice. If he didn't know better, he'd think…

He didn't know better. He knew nothing at all, Judah told himself, tiptoeing past her room. He had bigger fish to fry tonight than who was paying a nocturnal call on Fiona's personal secretary.

He sneaked past Fiona and Burke's room without any trouble, and flitted past the family library where they held their meetings, just in case any of the brothers were hanging out in there. One never knew where a Callahan might be loitering, and Judah didn't want to answer any questions.

Then he was out the door and into his truck. Not a soul would know he was laying his pride on the line.

"Where are we going?" Sam asked through the window of the truck, and Judah swallowed a good-size howl.

"*We* are going nowhere," he said. "*I'm* taking a short, *private* drive."

"Ah. To see Darla." Sam leaned his arms on the door. "You know what your problem is?"

"Tell me," Judah said. "I'm just dying to know."

"Your problem is that she's getting married in two days, and it's not to you. Getting that concussion is the best thing that ever happened to you."

"Why?" Judah asked, irritated.

"Because you need to be defending your castle, not riding rodeo."

"There's nothing to defend. I don't have a castle."

"If my lady was pregnant, there wouldn't be any discussion of her marrying another man. That sucker wouldn't dream of encroaching on my territory, because he'd know I'd knock his block off. In fact, my lady wouldn't be thinking about marrying another dude, because she'd be so wild to get into my bed." Sam gazed at him. "Like I said, you have a problem."

"Thanks for letting me know," Judah said, "because I hadn't figured that out on my own."

"You need to buck up. Now is the time for all good men to come to the aid of the party," Sam said.

"If there was a party to be had. Will you get out of my truck so I can go?" he demanded.

"You don't know of any women I could go carousing with tonight, do you?" his brother asked. "I'm in the mood for *looove*."

"Do I look like a dating service? Did you lose your little black book?" Judah was getting steamed. "Why would any sane woman want to carouse with you?"

Sam sighed. "This case is getting on my nerves. I could use a distraction."

Judah straightened. "Are there new developments?"

"Well, Bode's pretty endless with his tricks and appeals.

He's got a pretty seamy team of lawyers. And as you know, law isn't my strong suit."

Judah blinked. "You're the best lawyer around. No one bites the pants off the enemy like you. You're legendary for being a butt—ah, bulldog-like in the courtroom."

"But this is personal," Sam said, and Judah realized his brother needed to talk.

"Come on," Judah said. "Let's go carousing."

"Thought you'd never admit that you need a break from hearth and home." He got in the truck, grinning.

"Fiona's driving me nuts," Judah admitted. "She feeds me like a lost lamb."

"Ah, the benefits of home life." Sam looked at him. "So where are we going? Howling at Bode's bedroom window? I wouldn't mind giving the old goat a good fright."

"How about Darla's?" Judah turned down the drive.

"That doesn't sound like much fun unless the doc is there. We could run him off. *That* would be fun."

Judah's thoughts instantly ground to a halt. He'd never considered Darla might be having company. In his mind's eye, she was tucked up in her pristine bed waiting for his embrace—not the good doctor's.

"I'm not sure this is going to be as much fun as I thought it would be," he growled.

"Kind of tame stuff," Sam said, "when we should be painting 'Bode Sucks' on the water tower."

"That's kid's stuff." Judah frowned, thinking about Darla in bed with a rangy, loose-limbed retired bronc buster-turned-doctor. He had a horrible vision of Dr. Tunstall using his stethoscope to listen to Darla's heart going thumpety-thump for him—or even worse, listening to Judah's babies cooing inside Darla's nicely watermelon-shaped tummy. "I need something dangerous."

"Thinking about Darla sleeping with the good doc after the 'I do's' are said?" Sam asked, his tone commiserating.

Judah turned onto the main road. He was loaded for bear, his mood as territorial as he could ever remember it being. He was tired of Bode looming over them; he was tired of Tunstall, nice as he might be. But nice and in-the-way were two different things. "'Hang on to your ass, Fred,' to quote a favorite movie of mine. We're going to look in the face of danger with no regret."

Sam rubbed his hands together with enthusiasm. "Danger, here we come!"

Chapter Six

"This is your idea of dangerous?"

Sam glared at Judah as he held Jackie and Pete's girls, Molly and Elizabeth, on his lap. Judah waved a small stuffed pony he'd bought at the rodeo at the toddlers; he'd bought one for every Callahan child, passing them out like Santa Claus.

Judah grinned at Sam. "This is definitely my idea of dangerous. What did you have in mind, bro?"

Sam allowed little Fiona to crawl up in his lap. The triplets were dressed in their jammies, and old enough to realize they were being given a special treat of staying up past their bedtime. Jackie and Pete looked on fondly and with some amusement as Judah tried on daddy skills.

"I don't know," Sam said, "maybe lobbing a peck-happy chicken through Bode's bedroom window? Perhaps heading into town and seeing if we could rustle up some female attention? That's my idea of living on the edge. Of course you *are* darling," he said to mini-Fiona. "You're my niece, so what else would you be?"

"This is plenty dangerous for me," Judah said. "I'm not good with kids. I'm not cut out for fatherhood."

Pete laughed. "No one is. It just creeps up on you and you deal with it."

Jackie gave her husband a light smack on the arm. "You *are* cut out for being a dad," she told Judah. "You're a Callahan. All the brothers have a latent dad gene. I'm positive."

Judah grunted. "I can't convince Darla of that."

"But did you try?" Jackie asked, smiling. "Did you give her a reason to believe you were interested?"

"I suggested prenatal yoga. And vitamins. And good nutrition." Judah kissed his niece on the top of her head. "What more can I do?" He glanced to Jackie, puzzled, very aware that Pete was trying not to snicker.

"You offer to go *with* her to prenatal yoga," Jackie said gently. "And offer to cook those nutritious meals for her. Things like that. And offer to rub her belly."

"She won't let me rub anything of hers," Judah said morosely. "I'm pretty sure she thinks her pregnancy is a result of my, um, mishandling of the situation."

"It was," Sam said, unable to keep from tossing in his two cents.

"I used protection," Judah said defensively, frowning when everyone started laughing. "What?"

"You never read the box, did you?" Sam asked.

"The box of what?" Judah knew he was the butt of some secret joke, but he wasn't certain why. He'd come here for a little sympathy, and a bit of no-pressure, hands-on baby guidance. Not guffaws.

"Condoms," Sam said. "Creed gave us all joke condoms."

Judah blinked. "There's nothing funny about condoms."

Sam grinned at him. "You don't read directions."

"I'm a man of action," Judah shot back.

"And you fired away and asked questions later." Sam nodded. "That's the reason you're going to be a father."

"No," Judah said, "my box said something like 'For the Man Who Has Almost Everything.' *That* was the joke."

His family laughed harder. Judah shrugged. "It doesn't matter. Even if I begged to attend prenatal yoga, or promised to attend a cooking school for pregnant parents, Darla would still be determined to marry Doc Skin-and-Bones," he said. "You'd think she'd want a fellow with a little more muscle and meat to him. Those bronc busters always look like a string bean reverberating on the back of a horse to me. I'd rather my sons have a man to look up to who has muscles," he said with a sigh. "Strength."

"Meathead," Pete said, his tone kind. "You've got to quit letting Sidney bother you. Tell Darla—without being an ape—how you really feel about her."

"I don't know how not to be an ape." Judah stood, clapped his hat to his head, kissed the little girls goodbye. "Thank you for letting me be an uncle who doesn't call before he drops in at bedtime. I promise not to make a habit of it."

"Come anytime you like," Jackie said, giving him a hug. "We love you, Judah. We want you to be happy. You're a good man."

"Sometimes," Sam said. "When he's not a stupid man. Now can we go do something dangerous? Something that'll really rock the epicenter of wild-n-crazy? Like maybe drive to the Sonic, at least?"

Pete thumped Judah on the back. "It's always darkest before the dawn, dude. It'll work out."

"It's pretty damn dark out there," Judah said. "She's getting married in two days."

"You better rescue the princess *tout suite* then," Pete told him. "You can do it. You're a Callahan."

Judah nodded. "Thanks."

"Danger, here we come!" Sam said, kissing his nieces and hugging his sister-in-law goodbye.

Judah shook his head. Sam had no idea just what kind of danger lay in wait. And he couldn't tell him.

"YOU DID NOT INFORM ME that babysitting was your idea of dangerous," Sam said with a groan twenty minutes later, when they'd made their way to Creed's house. Sometimes Creed's sister-in-law Diane's three daughters stayed in the house with their little cousin, too, but tonight, it was just Creed and Aberdeen and their daughter, Joy Patrice.

"Not only is it dangerous," Judah said, holding out a stuffed pony for the baby, "it's essential. You should do one thing every day that scares you. It's important for your growth. And in my book, diapers are dangerous."

"Growth comes in the shape of luscious, eager females, too," Sam said, "but I can tell you're on a mission, so never mind." He sighed heavily and took the pony from Judah. "She's a baby. She can't hold a stuffed animal, idiot."

Judah gave Creed a stern eyeing. "Did you give us condoms that were basically party balloons?"

He grinned. "Seemed like a great groom's gift, as far as I was concerned."

"Why?" Judah demanded. "Do you mind me asking why?"

"To help you along. And clearly it did." Creed put on an innocent face. "It would be selfish of me to cheat you out of marital bliss. A little lambskin shouldn't stand between you and the most happiness you will ever know."

Judah snorted. "The mother of my children wants to marry someone else. Is that what you had in mind?"

"Now that sounds like a personal problem to me. Can't blame that on a neon party favor." Creed handed him a beer. "The box clearly said—"

"I know. I know. Only I'm not an owl. I don't see things in the dark, like very small print." Judah took the beer, more in the mood to bean his brother with it than to drink it. "I just thought that if a lady bothered to make love with a guy, then surely she had some kind of feelings for him."

Aberdeen looked at him with sympathy. "Darla does have feelings for you, Judah."

"What those feelings are could be anything," Creed said

unhelpfully, and Sam laughed. Judah hugged the baby in his arms, setting down his beer to gaze into her face. "Hey," he told her, "your uncles are pigs. But me, I'll rescue you. Don't worry, little princess. You'll always know Uncle Judah had your back."

"Knowing you," Creed said, "you've tried overwhelming Darla with your machismo. You've even given her the ol' I-know-what's-best-for-you treatment." He glanced at Judah. "So that only leaves romancing her socks off."

"Darla doesn't wear socks," Judah said, and everyone groaned.

"You have to go slowly for him," Sam said. "He's not the sharpest knife in the Callahan knife block."

"So, romance," Creed said, speaking slowly for Judah's benefit, as if he didn't know what to do with a woman, "is done with a gentle conductor's baton, a wand, if you will. Not a crashing bull-in-a-flower-bed thunderclap."

"Like you did with me?" Aberdeen said sweetly, and Judah and Sam hooted at their brother. "Judah, don't let Creed tell you he had all the answers, because he didn't."

"But he still won your heart," Judah said. "Though I don't know what you see in him."

That earned him a glare from Creed, which made Judah feel better.

"He won my heart by being persistent."

Creed stared at his wife. "No, I didn't. I won your heart by being the most awesome, irresistible—"

Aberdeen waved at Creed to be quiet. "Trust me, your brother made some mistakes in the wooing process. He was not a perfect prince. Nor was he a love machine, as he might lead you to believe."

Sam and Judah snickered as Creed was put in his place.

"But," Aberdeen said, "he hung in there, no matter what hoops I made him jump through, and I admired that. It made me realize that he actually loved me, in spite of all the doubts I had about us being together. And so he won my heart." She smiled at her husband, and Creed perked up like a plant in the sunshine.

"So how do I hang in there, when Darla doesn't even want me hanging in there? I left her a ring—a ring I was guaranteed would make a lady jump into my arms. And I got nothing," Judah said sadly. "Not even a phone call."

"Well," Aberdeen said, "perhaps it would be good to present your case in person."

"Yeah, dummy. You don't just leave a ring for a woman and hope she gets the clue. It takes more effort than that," Sam said. "Now can we go do something dangerous?"

Judah kissed his niece on the head. "Why is it that all we have on the ranch are baby girls?" he asked, thinking about the sons who would be in his arms before he knew it. A few months was nothing. He could hang in there.

He *could* hang in there. Just like Aberdeen said.

"We have baby girls," Creed said, "because it takes a real man to pack pink booties. Deal with it."

"WHERE'S THE DANGER?" Sam asked, when Judah pulled in front of Darla and Jackie's wedding shop. "This is just a dress store. It's a *wedding dress* store, but unless there's man-hunting brides around—and there's not, since it's nearly midnight—then I don't see the danger. Enlighten me."

Judah took a deep breath, wondering if he was going to be standing at an altar in two days or not. It was going to take everything he had to do it. "The danger is that you get to find a ride home," he told his brother. "I travel alone from here."

Sam gawked at him. "You would leave me in town with no ride?"

Judah nodded. "You wanted danger."

"I get it." Sam hopped out of the truck, wearing a sour expression. "This is not my idea of danger."

"Yes, but your day is coming." Judah waved at his brother. "I'm going to go find an ex-nurse and see if she wants to take my temperature."

"Huh," Sam said, "good luck with that."

He loped off, heading toward the town's only secret night spot, in the back of Banger's Bait and Tackle. Judah drove away, thinking about everything he'd seen in his brothers' homes. It was true that they probably hadn't had the smoothest routes to the altar. They were certainly not hard-core princes.

But they had made it across the finish line.

And that's where Judah wanted to be.

Chapter Seven

It was rude to pay a visit at midnight, particularly without calling first, but time was of the essence. Judah figured he could blame his lack of manners on his nonexistent concussion, which he considered overcautiousness, and maybe even passive-aggressiveness, on Sidney's part. The bronc buster had known that Judah was winning. He hadn't wanted to give his rival any reason to look like a hero, so he'd scratched Judah.

Therefore, it was completely legit to be here. And there was a lamp shining in the window, so a tap on the door would let him know whether Darla wanted company.

There were no vehicles in the drive, and Judah figured she had no nocturnal guest sleeping over. "That's a good thing," he murmured. "I would have hated to toss ol' Sid out on his bony butt."

He knocked.

"Who is it?" Darla asked, and Judah took a deep breath.

"The father of your children."

"Judah," Darla said through the door, "it's late. I have work tomorrow, and I have a doctor's appointment. I don't have time for fun and games."

Fun and games? Was that how she saw him? "I could play the pity card and tell you I had to scratch from the rodeo due to a slight concussion, and that only a nurse would understand, but—"

The door opened. She looked out at him, her expression wary. "Did you really?"

"Yes. And no. I actually don't think I hit my head, but Tunstall scratched me, and the E.R. said I had a hairline concussion, or stage one. Something like that—I wasn't paying attention." He shrugged. "I think it was Tunstall's evil plot to get me out of the rodeo."

She shook her head. "Sidney's not like that."

"I was fine," Judah insisted. "I've ridden with worse injuries."

She sighed and opened the door. "Come in, but only for five minutes."

He took off his hat and sat awkwardly on the sofa. She looked so cute in her blue robe and little flip-flops. Okay, maybe those weren't sex-goddess garments, but he liked her comfy. It felt homelike here. "This is a nice place."

"No room at the inn." She crossed her arms. "Judah, what did you want to talk about?"

He forced himself to pay attention to why he'd come in the first place. "I don't think you should get married. It's too soon. You could be making the biggest mistake of your life, which will affect my sons."

She frowned. "I don't know the sex of my children, because I haven't asked the doctor. I don't want to know until they're born. So please don't refer to them as males."

"They'll be boys," Judah said. "Pete and Creed might not be capable of manly offspring, but I am."

Darla sighed. "Judah, I'm getting married in two days. Whatever you think about what I'm doing isn't important."

"Can I get a restraining order or something?" Judah pondered this. "There has to be a law where a man can stop a woman from making a foolish mistake in his sons' lives."

Her frown deepened. He could see he'd landed in deep cow droppings with that tack. He decided to change course before he got thrown out on his ear. "What I'm trying to say, Darla, is that I don't think you've given us a chance."

Once he'd said it, it was like a cork popping out of a bottle. "We've started off on the wrong foot for a number of reasons, but there's a spark between us."

"And we should blow on that spark and see if it bursts into flame or goes out altogether?" Darla didn't look convinced. "Judah, there isn't one compelling reason you can offer for me to call off my wedding. I'm not convinced you and I have any sparks, but where you're concerned, I'm pretty flame-resistant."

Well, wasn't that just a pearl every man wanted to hear falling from his beloved's sweet lips? She didn't think there were sparks.

There was only one thing to do. He could be run off by his pumpkin's frosty ways, or he could be a fireman.

He pulled Darla into his lap and said, "I don't know why you're fighting so hard. Maybe you just like a chase. But I'm good at running. And as long as I know you haven't returned my ring, I'm going to believe that you're just fighting your practical side."

She slid from his lap onto the sofa. "You make me sound… like a tease."

He kissed her neck. "Mmm, you smell delicious. And don't put words in my mouth. You're a hot little number, Darla Cameron, and I'm not afraid of a little teasing. You tease me all you like, and I'll tease you back. Although, that night we shared might have been a one-off, come to think of it," he said, angling for a kiss, which he adroitly stole. He noticed she wasn't exactly fighting him. "What's holding us back from having a really kinky lovefest, anyway? Just me and you and a bowl of fruit, maybe?"

"Sidney."

Judah raised a brow. "Didn't you tell me that you and Tunstall aren't exactly burning holes in the bedsheets?"

She stiffened like a dress mannequin with a pole up its back. "That isn't how I phrased it, thank you, speaking of putting words in someone's mouth."

He leaned back comfortably against the sofa and indicated she should go on with her explanation. "I think a woman who is planning on a sexless marriage—a business arrangement—probably has a very good reason for locking herself in a gilded cage."

"You don't know everything," Darla said, "and it's really none of your affair. Now, if you don't mind, I have to be at work early in the morning. We have a shipment of gowns arriving."

He nodded. "And you need all the beauty sleep you can get before the wedding. I understand. It's a bride thing." He stood. "Not that I think Tunstall's much of a catch, but—"

"It doesn't matter what you think," Darla said. "Anyway, what's wrong with him?"

"Nothing," Judah said, a tad too quickly. "Nothing at all."

"You're just annoyed because he made you scratch. That's why you're here, isn't it?"

"No," Judah said, "I'm here to kiss you good night."

He kissed Darla like he might not ever kiss her again. He held her, framing her face with his hands, touching her skin, telling her with his kisses how he felt about her. He couldn't bear the thought of her marrying another man. Darla belonged with him, and he couldn't imagine why she didn't see it the same way he did. He kissed Darla with his whole heart and soul, thrilled to finally have her in his arms. So it was a horrible shock to his soul when banging erupted on the front door.

Darla jumped away from him as if she'd been zapped by a cattle prod. "Who is it?"

"Sidney."

"He can't find you here!" She started shooing Judah toward the bedroom.

"I'm not hiding," he declared. "But even if I would hide like a weasel, don't you think the bedroom is the last place he'd want to find me?"

Darla shook her head. "He won't come in here. Don't move! If you do, I swear I'll...you'll wish you only had a slight concussion!" She closed the bedroom door.

Judah shrugged. "Well, this wasn't how I planned to get in here," he said to himself, "but I'm okay with it." He pulled off his boots, his shirt, his jeans, his socks, hesitated at the black Polo briefs, then shrugged and tossed them on the pile, too. What the hell. He didn't sleep in anything at home; no reason to stand on ceremony now. No telling how long Boy Wonder would be pressing his case with his not-gonna-be-bride, so Judah slid into Darla's bed wearing nothing but a grin.

"Now *this* is living dangerously," he said in the dark, briefly wondering if Sam had made it home and was as comfortable as Judah was at this very moment. Impossible. This bed—Darla's bed—was simply the best place to be in Diablo. And then Judah fell asleep in Darla's soft, cozy, clean smelling sheets, wondering when she'd remember that Judah's truck was parked out front where even Tunstall couldn't miss it.

Sam was right. It was huge fun living dangerously.

"DO YOU HAVE COMPANY?" Sidney asked, and Darla glanced nervously at the bedroom door. She wasn't certain she could trust Judah not to come popping out like a jack-in-the-box to annoy Sidney. Even now, she was pretty sure Judah had his big ear pressed flat to the door, listening to every word, carefully choosing his moment to spring.

"I actually do have company," she said, unable to lie to Sidney. He'd been too kind to her. He really was a nice man, and they made a good team. Sometimes she suspected that he felt a little more than friendly toward her, and then other times he was strictly professional.

Yet Judah wouldn't play nice and understand the unique situation she was in. *Stubborn ass.*

"Do you mind me asking who it is?" Sidney asked, and Darla sighed.

"It's Judah."

"He's in there?" Sidney jerked his head toward her bedroom.

"He'd be happy to come out, if you want. I told him to go in there while you were here. I wasn't aware you'd planned to stop by." She looked at him, gauging his reaction, but he seemed like the Sidney of always, calm and unconcerned.

Not in love with her. Which was a relief.

"No." Sidney sat on the sofa, making himself comfortable. "I'm happy for him to cower in there if you're okay with it."

Darla sat at the other end of the sofa. "So what's on your mind?"

"I just want to make certain you still want to go through with this, now that Judah knows he's the father." Sidney looked at her. "I'd completely understand if you feel that your circumstances have changed."

"There's nothing between Judah and me," Darla said. "He wants to be a father to his children, which I'm grateful for. But there's no reason…" She stopped, thinking about the beautiful diamond ring Judah had given her. She remembered the satiny feel of the magic wedding gown as she'd slipped it on. It had felt so right, so real, like she was meant to wear it and be a beloved bride.

Then she thought about Judah standing behind her in the mirror, his handsome face gazing at her with love and passion—yes, she'd seen passion in those dark blue eyes—and she shivered. He'd made love to her with an intensity that had rocked her. She knew that side of Judah Callahan.

But not much else. And she didn't want a man who simply felt that she should be his because he'd made children with her. "Nothing needs to change between us, Sidney. You still need a wife to satisfy your inheritance, and I'm more than willing to be a stand-in."

Sidney looked as if he was about to say something, then closed his mouth. His lips, she noticed, weren't full and capable of being demanding—like Judah's. Sidney's lips were thinner, almost nonexistent, as if he was used to holding back his emotions a lot. She considered his dark brown hair, dark eyes, kind face. "Sidney, why haven't you ever married, anyway?"

He shrugged. "I'm always on the road. I have a house that's nice enough, but no woman wants to go home alone at night for months on end."

"That's true, I guess." Darla thought about how nice it was that Judah was so close to his family. They were always around. Sometimes they aggravated each other, but most of the time it was obvious that they all loved each other a lot.

She really wanted a big family for her babies.

"I guess I'll be alone much of the time," she murmured.

He winced. "If you marry me, that's unfortunately part of the deal. I will take very good care of you, when I'm around. And financially you won't lack for anything. Nor will your children, whom I'm willing to adopt as my own."

She took a deep breath. She really didn't need to be "taken care of," as nice as Sidney was trying to be. She'd always taken care of herself just fine. What she really wanted was a father for her babies, a name for them to own, so that they wouldn't grow up wondering why they'd had no daddy.

But she hadn't counted on Judah being so determined to be a father. He was Mr. Footloose, Mr. Don't-Tie-Me-Down.

The huge diamond he'd bought her almost made her change her opinion of him.

Almost.

She owed it to the children to find out. "I think," Darla said softly, "maybe I'd better wait and see how this turns out, Sidney." She looked at him. "I'm so sorry. I hope you can forgive me."

He shrugged. "Nothing to forgive. I completely understand. It's why I came out tonight."

She nodded. "You're a good doctor. And a good man."

"I know," he said, standing. "You've heard that good guys always win, haven't you?"

She smiled. "It's true. You'll win."

He pressed a gentle kiss against her knuckles. "I have half a mind to go in there and tell Judah that I lied about his concussion."

She blinked. "You did?"

"I said I thought he had one. I felt it was important to get him off the road. The hospital never really found anything, either. They just told him he needed rest. He ran with the advice—quickly, I might add, right to your door." Sidney glanced toward the bedroom. "Part of me wants to go in there and tell him we've decided to elope tonight, and would he mind keeping an eye on the house while we're gone." He grinned at Darla. "What do you think he'd say?"

"I don't know," she answered.

"I do." Sidney smiled at her, tipped his hat and left. She listened as his truck gunned to life and he drove away.

Then she went to her bedroom, opening the door abruptly just in case Judah did have his ear pressed tight to it. She fully intended to smack him a good one for being so nosy.

But he was asleep in her bed—nude, judging by the pile

of clothes on the floor. And obviously not worried one bit by what was transpiring in the other room.

It stung. He could have been pacing a little at least.

All he really wanted was to be a bad-ass. And it wasn't going to work with her.

But here they were, bound together. She placed a hand on her belly.

Her babies' father was sleeping blissfully, unconcerned that he did not love their mother. But he would do his duty, just like any of the Callahans would.

There was only one option that would solve their dilemma.

Chapter Eight

Dear Judah,
You and I aren't in love. You want to get married because of the babies, but I have a proposal of my own for you. Let's agree to stay together until after the twins are born, and then we'll reevaluate the situation. That's the best deal I can come up with right now, because I really don't think we're meant for each other as married partners. But we'll try it your way for the sake of the children, if only temporarily. If you agree to a divorce after the babies are born, I'll be at the altar in two days, ready to say I do.
Darla

She put the letter in an envelope, decided to leave it on the kitchen counter where Judah would easily find it. She laid his beautiful ring beside the letter. The diamond caught the light from the overhead hanging fixture, sending prisms dancing over the counter. Her breath caught just looking at it. A princess would wear such a lovely ring.

She was not a princess. She was an unwed mother with a scoundrel for a one-night-stand daddy. "Oh, boy," she murmured, and closed her eyes for a moment. Did she really want to be married only until the children were born? It sounded so prenup, so planned.

At least she was giving him the freedom to leave. And for the sake of her pride, she had to know that he had an escape hatch built in to their agreement. She felt tears pool behind her eyes, told herself she'd spent far too much time staring at dreamy white gowns. She'd gone from a no-nonsense nurse to a woman who dreamed fairy-tale dreams—and it hurt.

Strong arms closed around her, making her jump. Warm lips pressed to the back of her neck, sending sizzles zipping along her skin.

"Is that a Dear John letter you're leaving me?" Judah asked against her nape, and Darla closed her eyes.

"Not exactly." His hard body pressed against her and her knees went weak. "Please tell me you're wearing something."

He kissed the side of her neck. "I think you'd be very disappointed if I was wearing clothes, Darla. You don't have to pretend you're a straight-laced nurse who'll read me the riot act for making a pass at you. Although if I was one of your patients, I definitely would have tried—"

"Judah," Darla said, unable to think about where he was going with that while he was driving her out of her mind with kisses. "I could have a better conversation with you if you weren't nude."

"I don't want to chitchat, doll. I want to hold you and make you scream like a wildcat. Which I know you can do very well." He nipped her shoulder lightly, then ran a tongue over the spot he'd bitten. "The question is, are Dear John letters supposed to be written on pink stationary with a purple pen? It seems to send a romantic signal, dressing it up like that. Black and white would be a lot more impersonal for bad news, I would think. But I wouldn't know," he added, his voice husky. "I have to admit no lady of my acquaintance has ever tried to write me off."

"I'm sure." Darla didn't dare turn around. He was rascal enough to not have a stitch on, and she didn't want to see his firm, well-muscled body. She wasn't strong enough to deny herself a naked Judah whose body was carved by a master sculptor.

"Where's the good doc?" he asked, his breath warm against her neck, tickling the tiny hairs at her nape. "Not trusting me alone with the treasure, is he?"

"Judah, I'm not treasure. And yes, Sidney would trust me. Totally."

"I guess he was trusting you when you sneaked into my room that night?"

She swallowed. "Sidney…Sidney and I aren't getting married anymore. So quit bothering me about him. And please put something on! And leave. I want you to leave."

He took the envelope from her fingers. "Is that what this says? Go away, big bad wolf, and never come back?"

She didn't nod, because she hadn't written anything of the sort. Now she felt foolish for what she had written. Why hadn't she realized how unwise it was to try to bargain with a devil? She tried to snatch the envelope away from him, but Judah eluded her easily.

"Ah," he said, running the envelope down her back so it rasped along her zipper, "you don't want me to read something that has my name on it? I find that strange, Darla Cameron. And one thing you usually aren't is strange."

"Judah, there is a robe in my closet. If you'll at least put on a robe, we can have an adult conversation."

"Now, my love," he said, kissing the shell of her ear, "being an adult is one thing no one's ever accused me of. Besides, I like your backside so much. I remember it fondly."

She closed her eyes, wishing she wasn't pressed against the kitchen counter. He'd teased her enough, she decided. She was going to turn around, was going to face this strong, naked man and tell him she'd changed her mind. She just wanted her letter back, and to give up her unwise attempt at taming this lion.

She was melting, knowing full well what wonderful pleasures lay in store for her if she just gave in.

She couldn't.

Whirling around, she kept her eyes forcefully averted from the masculine glory. "Judah, give me back that envelope right now." Her gaze ran the length of him in astonishment. "You're not naked! You're fully dressed!"

"Disappointed?" he asked, grinning as he stole a kiss. "Sorry about that, babe, but I've got to go. Duty calls back at the ranch. Sleep well." He waved the envelope at her before tucking it in his shirt pocket. "I'll save this for my nightly bedtime reading. I'm sure it'll prove to be interesting, even fascinating. I never expected a letter from my lady." He winked at her, so devil-may-care it was maddening.

"I want it back!"

"Ah, no. I bid you good night. I would stay, sugar, but at this hour, I'm afraid I only have one thing on my mind. And I'm sure you know what that is." He stole another kiss and departed, leaving Darla lathered up and pink-cheeked.

She spun around and saw that the ring was still there, sparkling on the counter. He knew she wanted it. He knew it tempted her. He knew *he* tempted her.

In fact, she was drowning in temptation.

There was nothing she wanted to do more than run after him and beg him to come back, spend the night with her, make love to her. He probably knew that about her, too. He'd so shamelessly teased her about his nudity, making her think about him naked, making her remember. Oh, he was baiting her, and it was working.

She didn't know how she was going to sleep tonight.

"WELL, IF IT ISN'T Roughriding Romeo," Sam said when Judah dragged himself into the bunkhouse well after midnight. "Mr. Danger himself."

"Glad you made it home, bro. I figured you would." Judah hung his hat on the hook in the mudroom and looked at his brothers in front of the fireplace. Jonas, Rafe and Sam stared at him with raised brows and expectant expressions.

"So, did you find any danger?" Sam asked.

"Nope," Judah said, "nothing but lambs and cotton candy in my world."

"What's that pink thing poking out of your shirt?" Jonas asked.

"This," Judah said proudly, "is my first Dear John letter."

"Nothing to brag about there," Rafe said. "You weren't even a 'dear' as far as Darla was concerned in the first place. So if she's writing you off, you're going backward, bro."

"This Dear John letter means," Judah said, running it under his nose to smell the scent of Darla's perfume, "that she cares about me enough to try to run me off. She's fighting it, brothers, every step of the way. And that's the way I like my lady."

"Reluctant? Distant? Icy, even?" Sam said. "You always were the peculiar one of us."

"Darla's none of the above." Judah threw himself on the sofa lengthwise, cradling his head on a sofa pillow. "She's fighting herself. And she's losing."

"You can tell all that without even opening the letter? Maybe you've picked up some of Sabrina's psychic skills. But I advise you to read it before you go crowing about how hot your runaway bride is for you," Jonas said.

"She won't run from our wedding, that's for sure. She'll be too practical for that. I'm a catch." Judah shrugged and tore open the envelope to hoots from his brothers, pulling out the letter to read it. "This is better news than I'd hoped, even," he murmured. "She's given the skinny bronc buster the wave-off."

"Really?" Sam perked up. "He's cleared the field for you?"

"And she's planning on marrying me in two days. I told

you!" Judah looked up at his brothers in triumph. "I hope I still fit in my tux."

"Dummy," Rafe said. "Sidney wasn't going to wear a tux. Why should you?"

"Why not? It's a special occasion. It calls for a tux." Judah was pretty certain that in spite of her protestations to the contrary, he and Darla would be married forever. He planned to make rock-solid vows in two days, and no way was he ever letting her give him the slip like she'd given Tunstall. Oh, she might think that was what she wanted, and certainly he would agree to her darling little last-ditch attempt to keep herself from falling head over heels in love with him. But this agreement she wanted bought him time. And he could do a whole lot of convincing in four or five months. Judah squinted at the ceiling. "Which one of you dunces wants to be my best man?"

"I'm not feeling it," Jonas said. "Something tells me nothing good can come of marrying a woman who's Miss Reluctant."

"I'm telling you she wants me. Read it for yourself." He handed the letter to Jonas, who snatched it and read it before passing it to his brothers. They all looked at him with worried expressions. Judah shrugged at their hangdog faces. "Don't worry. She's crazy about me."

Rafe sighed. "If I have to, I'll be the sacrificial lamb who stands next to you at the altar while you sign on to get burned a few months hence. But it doesn't feel like happy ever after to me."

"Thanks, tough guy." Judah closed his eyes, annoyed. He waved the letter in the air again. "This is my ticket, my golden chance, my checkmate, if you will. I win."

"We see," Sam said. "We see that you're nuts. Darla's telling you up front she has every intention of marrying you so her babies will have a name. Then she's divorcing you, dude."

"So? I'd rather her marriage-of-convenience be with me than with Sidney. That puts me in her bed, and therefore, in medal contention."

"You think of everything in terms of winning or losing," Sam said. "I don't know if that's healthy."

"Yeah," Rafe said, "what if Darla gives you the boot, as per this agreement? Don't you have to be a gentleman and honor that? Or else it's not valid. She doesn't have to say yes until you agree."

Judah shrugged. "Just be ready in two days to toss birdseed, bros. That's your only job."

His brothers grimaced, then went back to what they'd been doing, which looked to be high-stakes, boring Scrabble. Judah smiled to himself. They had no idea that he had everything completely under control. And they could keep their bachelor jealousy to themselves. He was going to be in contention for Fiona's ranch-o-rama, and they weren't.

Darla was going to be Mrs. Callahan, and he was going to be the hero with strong boys who'd ride rodeo just like him. A bull rider and his bundles of joy—how great was that? He knew all about what Darla wanted, and what the practical side of her wanted was a fab dad. Once she saw how great he was with the little lads, she'd never want to let him go.

Just two days.

It seemed like forever.

Chapter Nine

"I'm worried about Judah," Jonas said, after Judah had conked out. "He thinks he's got this all planned down to a script, but I think the situation's more explosive than he realizes." Jonas squinted at the Scrabble board, considering his options.

Rafe nodded. "I was thinking the same thing."

"Still," Sam said, "it's his business if he wants to get burned like an onion on a grill. We can't save him from being stupid."

"The problem," Jonas said, glancing over at the peacefully snoring Judah, "is that he believes he can convince Darla that she loves him. The two of them have lived in the same town almost all their lives, and never even played doctor with each other."

Rafe and Sam blinked at him. "Doctor?" Sam said.

"Yeah." Jonas grimaced. "You know. Doctor."

Rafe considered that. "I've never played doctor with any of the girls in this town. Spin the bottle, maybe. Pin the tail on the donkey, definitely." He frowned at Jonas. "You don't strike me as the type to play doctor, Jonas."

Sam snickered. "I played doctor. I also got slapped. Ah, good times." He looked at Jonas. "Is that why you became a doctor, because you liked playing it so much?"

"No," Jonas said, "I became a doctor because I'm smart, and I like helping people. I like puzzles."

"It had nothing to do with beautiful nurses," Rafe said. "Good thing, too, or that would have been a waste of your time, considering you've never brought a beautiful nurse home. Or any nurse."

Jonas sighed. "All I was trying to say is that Judah and Darla never had the hots for each other before. So why get married?" He glared at his brothers. "There, was that plain enough for you boobs?"

"Plain enough for me," Rafe said. "I don't think we can save him, though. He's on a mission to marry."

"I think we should test that mission," Jonas said, "to make certain true love exists. After all, it's easier to call off a wedding than to get a divorce later on. Some people have marital counseling, you know, to help them decide if they're on a successful path with their chosen—"

"Bah," Sam said. "I say let him fall on his face."

Jonas looked at Rafe. "That leaves you the deciding vote."

Rafe appeared troubled. "I see your point about saving pain for him and for Darla and for the children later by not putting them through a divorce. I also see Sam's point about it being Judah's business what he does. How exactly do you plan to test this marriage-of-convenience adventure?"

"Simple," Jonas said. "We tell Judah we think he's making a mistake. We just be honest. Nothing underhanded, just plain old honesty."

Rafe shook his head. "I don't want to be punched, thank you."

"Me, neither," Sam said. "I'm the brains of this outfit, you know. I'm trying to save us from Bode. Since it's your idea, it should probably be you, Jonas. You are eldest, after all."

"And I'm the surgeon," Jonas said, "who will stitch Rafe up when he busts his lip on Judah's knuckles."

Rafe shrugged. "Anyway, I still say the deciding factor is it's his life. The truth is, those babies do need a name. And it is all Creed's fault that a Callahan got Darla into this mess, so a Callahan should bail her out."

Sam and Jonas looked at him. Then they looked at Judah, who was snoring, his chin practically pointing toward the ceiling.

"He really isn't much of a catch," Rafe said. "I guess if all Darla needs is a name for her children, I can do the marriage-of-convenience thing as well as anybody. If it would save Darla from making a disastrous mistake."

"You mean Judah," Sam said.

"I mean Darla," Rafe retorted. "He really isn't much of a catch, like I said."

They sat silently, mulling over the situation. Then Jonas leaned over, kicked at Judah's leg with his boot. Judah's eyes snapped open.

"What?" he said. "Are you losers still playing Scrabble? Don't you know how to spell a word longer than three letters?"

"Rafe has something to tell you," Jonas said.

Rafe looked miserable. "We think marrying in haste means repenting in leisure."

"Whatever." Judah moved his hat down over his eyes and shifted to a more comfortable position on the leather couch.

"We think," Rafe said, trying again bravely, "that marriage isn't your style. You're more of a drifter."

"No, I'm not," Judah said from under the hat. "I'm a pragmatic romantic."

They went dead silent for a moment. He grinned, but the felt of his Stetson covering his face kept them from knowing he was laughing at them. They thought they were being so Fiona, but they weren't. No one could plot like Fiona, and Judah had learned at her knee.

"I'm going to tell Darla I'm willing to marry her so her babies will have a name," Rafe said.

Judah rolled his eyes. "You do that."

Silence met his pronouncement. Judah snickered. His brothers were always trying to help, though not successfully, and he had to admire their ham-handed ways.

"You don't mind?" Rafe asked, sounding a little less sure of himself.

"Nope," Judah said. "Have at it."

"I vote we resume this game later," Jonas said, and Sam said, "A fine idea, since Rafe has to be somewhere."

Sam said it importantly, as if Rafe was about to run right over and pop the question to Darla. *These goofballs,* Judah thought. *I don't know what they're up to, but Darla would never want to marry anyone but me. She wants me bad.*

"Okay," Rafe said, "see you later."

The door opened, and Judah heard boots moving out the door. "Called your bluff, didn't I?" he said, sliding the hat from his face. He was alone. They'd gone, ostensibly to scare him into thinking Rafe was actually heading off to save Judah's princess from her self-declared dilemma. But Darla wanted only one cowboy. *And that's me,* he assured himself.

He glanced over at the Scrabble board, seeing a lack of imagination in the chosen spellings. "'Marriage, wife, convenience, bad idea,'" he said out loud, eyeing the tiles. "Oh, very funny. You guys are a laugh a minute." He went back to sleep, completely unconcerned. He had everything under control.

"MARRY YOU?" Darla asked twenty minutes later, when Rafe had hotfooted it over to her house and banged on her door. He'd told her he'd just left Judah, after telling him he was going to propose. Darla didn't know what to think about the Callahans anymore, except that maybe they were just as crazy as everyone said. "Why would I want to marry you?"

"You'd like me better in the temporary sense," Rafe said,

"and after all, it was my twin's gag gift that got you into this dilemma. I feel a certain irony to putting matters right."

She frowned, wondering why Judah hadn't told her about a gag gift. "Gag gift?"

Rafe nodded. "Judah didn't tell you?"

She shook her head.

"Creed gave us all prank condoms as groom gifts. Clearly, the joke was on Judah." Rafe stood straighter. "Like I said, I'm here to put things right."

Darla's heart was sinking. "Judah didn't mind you proposing to me?"

Rafe shook his head. "No, he said to have at it."

Darla wondered what new game Judah had up his sleeve. Her pride came to the fore as she said, "I don't understand why this would solve anything."

"Well, if it's a temporary situation you're looking for, and I guess it is, due to the pink ultimatum you gave Judah, it would be better to marry me, because I am all about temporary. Short Term is my middle name. In fact, No Term is what they should have named me—"

"You don't think Judah will honor the divorce?"

"Nope," Rafe said. "We're territorial in my family. He's not going to give you up once he has those little cherubs under his control. I mean his, uh, loving guidance."

Darla considered that. "But Judah doesn't love me."

Rafe shrugged. "Hasn't he told you that he does?"

"No." Darla looked at Rafe. "I can raise these children on my own. I don't need anyone to help me with that. I want to marry for love."

"I know. But it may not happen." He looked properly saddened by this revelation, which didn't make her feel any better. "As you know, you're like a sister to me. I've always loved all women, but you have a special place in my heart. I don't want to see you get hurt." Rafe wondered if he was carrying his role a little too far. The more he talked, the more he believed his story. The truth was, Darla and Judah didn't love each other; getting a divorce after the babies were born was going to hurt them, their children and the family.

But if Rafe married Darla, and she knew he was doing it to give her children a name, then there was no ulterior motive. But there was the small matter of him carrying a super-secret torch for Judge Julie, Bode's daughter. He sighed deeply.

"Darla, I'm here for you if you don't want to marry Judah, and probably no sane woman would want to, I suppose."

"I guess you're right," Darla said, thinking that she'd have loved to marry Judah, if things had been different. If they'd fallen in love gently and slowly, finding each other of their own will and choosing, not this slamming together of their separate galaxies. "It's nice of you to offer, Rafe, but actually, I don't want to marry you, either."

He blinked. "Either?"

She sighed. "No. I don't want to marry you, of course, because you're right. You are a brother to me. And I don't want to marry Judah. I'd always feel like the wallflower that got asked to dance because the guy felt sorry for her." She felt tears prickle her eyes, but stood her ground. "Thank you for coming by, Rafe. It's been helpful."

"It has?" Rafe wasn't certain the conversation hadn't gone wildly off the guided track. She wasn't supposed to be saying she didn't want either of them. She was supposed to insist that Judah was the only man for her, once she realized it was true. Clearly, she'd realized something of a totally different sort. "So what are you going to do?"

Darla smiled. "What I should have done all along."

"I HAVE TO GIVE THIS BACK to you," Darla said, laying the magic wedding dress carefully over the bed in Sabrina's room at Rancho Diablo. "It's lovely." She gave Sabrina a smile she didn't realize was sad until she felt it on her face. "Thank you for offering it to us. Jackie felt like a princess when she wore it to her wedding."

Sabrina studied Darla. "Do you want to talk about it?"

"There's nothing to talk about. I think our customers just aren't looking for gowns that are quite so vintage."

"I meant do you want to talk about your wedding? Or anything else?"

Darla shook her head. "There won't be a wedding. For one thing, Sidney and I have decided to remain simply friends."

"And Judah?"

"Judah and I have a complicated situation. We're still trying to figure out how to say hello to each other without feeling awkward."

"Is there anything I can do?"

Darla shook her head again. "I don't think so. Callahans are different types to deal with, as I'm sure you know."

Sabrina smiled. "It's true."

"Do you think you and Jonas will ever—"

"No." Sabrina shook her own head. "You and Judah do not have the market cornered on awkward."

Darla smiled. "Why that makes me feel better, I don't know."

"Misery loves company."

Sabrina hung the gown in her closet, closing it away. Darla fancied she could still hear the lovely song of its allure calling to her. It was like looking at a sparkling diamond a woman dreamed of one day owning—

"Oh!" Darla jumped to her feet. "I'm sorry to cut this short. I just remembered something I have to do."

Sabrina nodded. "Judah's in the bunkhouse. And if you change your mind about the dress, it'll be here, ready to go on short notice."

"Thanks," Darla said, thinking that short notice and

her wedding would never go together. She'd learned about being hasty—and next time, if there ever was a next time she planned a wedding, she was taking the long route.

"SO THEN WHAT DID SHE SAY?" Jonas asked. Sam was glued to Rafe's every word. They sat around the Scrabble board, but they weren't playing. Judah was nowhere to be found. There were chores that had to be done—ASAP—but at the moment, Jonas and Sam were spellbound by Rafe's bungling of the Darla Problem.

"She said she didn't want to marry me or Judah," Rafe said. "She was pretty definite about it, too."

"Judah's going to kill you," Sam said. "You were supposed to help Darla see that Judah is the only man for her."

"She doesn't think like most women," Rafe said in his defense. "She's pretty independent. And I think Judah annoys her fiercely."

"What does that have to do with anything?" Jonas demanded. "We don't care if she's annoyed. We care that she takes Judah off our hands and keeps him forever."

"It was scary," Rafe said. "For a minute, I thought she was going to take me up on my offer." He shuddered. "I don't think Judah understands how thin a thread he's hanging by with Darla."

"This isn't good." Jonas considered the information about Judah's precarious nuptials. "We could talk to Fiona, tell her that the lovebirds are planning to get a divorce *inmediatamente.* That would frost her cookies. I think that falls under the heading of no fake marriages, and puts him out of contention for the ranch. She won't be happy."

Sam swallowed. "I've got to have a fake marriage if I play the game. I'm never letting a woman lead me around by the nose."

Rafe sighed. "If you don't think that women are doing that every day of your life already, you're dumb."

Sam sniffed. "Well, we can't tell Fiona. She'd just throw a party. That's her answer for everything. Party, party. It's her stress buster."

"Any news on the filing?" Jonas asked. "What's the update on our legal status?"

Sam shrugged. "We could stand for Judah to get married and populate this joint. If we had a small city of kiddies here, maybe we could make a case that we are the people. The people would be best served by us keeping the ranch and opening an elementary school for the community. Something like that, anyway."

Rafe straightened. "That's a great idea. We need an elementary school. I like kids. I like school bells. Let's build a school with a school bell!"

Jonas sighed. "Let's not put the bell before the babies, all right? First we have to get Judah to slide over home plate."

"Yeah," Rafe said, "and since he told me I could marry the mother of his children, I'm pretty sure he's not in love. It would stand to reason."

"Yeah," Sam agreed. "You wouldn't even need a lawyer to make that case. If I was in love with a woman, I wouldn't let any of you fatheads near her. Probably not even to offer her a glass of water."

"You're selfish, though," Jonas said. "Maybe Judah is more generous."

His brothers blew a collective raspberry at him.

"Judah's not in love," Sam said, "or he would have kicked Rafe's ass when he told him he was going to pop the question to Darla."

"Yeah," Rafe said, "and my ass is un-kicked. It's depressing."

"Look at that," Jonas said, waving at his brothers to come

to the bunkhouse window. "Darla just came out of the house. She's heading this way." He glanced at Rafe. "Suppose she's changed her mind about you?"

"Hide me," Rafe said. "She's got a gleam in her eye that doesn't bode well."

"Where's Judah?" Jonas asked. "We need him front and center to catch this incoming fireball."

"Probably in the tub with his rubber ducky. How would I know?" Sam asked.

"Let's sneak out the back," Jonas said. "They'll find their way to each other eventually, and I don't want to be in the path of love."

"Or not," Rafe said. "Last one out the back door has to tell Fiona we screwed up Judah's life."

The brothers did their best Three Stooges impersonation getting out the door. Judah heard the back door slam, looked out his bedroom window in time to see the trio of siblings running for the barn.

"Immature," he muttered, pulling on a shirt. "Always competing."

"Judah?" a female voice called, and he grinned. *I knew that little gal couldn't resist me.*

"Hi," he said, framing himself in the bedroom doorway. "Little Red Riding Hood must be looking for her wolf," he said, taking Darla by the hand and tugging her into his room. He locked the door. "Lucky for you, I just happen to be *very* hungry."

Chapter Ten

"Very funny." Darla swallowed her unease. "I'll wait out in the den."

"Don't be scared. I'll be good to you. No biting."

Warily, she removed her hand from his. She hesitated to be anyplace that contained Judah and a bed, but he was hardly going to jump on her and eat her like a chocolate bunny. As he said, no biting.

"I brought you this," she said, trying not to look at him as she set his ring on the nightstand. She glanced around, curious in spite of herself. His bunkhouse room was sparsely furnished, but he kept it neat. The quilt on the bed was vintage, a beautiful patchwork pattern that must have taken months. Someone had cared deeply about the project. But Darla could hardly pay attention to the room's decor when Judah's shirt was open and he was zipping up his work jeans. She wished she hadn't accepted his invitation to enter his lair.

Bedroom. It was just four walls. Four walls and a bed where they could be together.

There was a time she'd dreamed of nothing more.

"I'm not marrying you, Judah," Darla said, and he grinned at her, a slow, confident grin that unsettled her and got her off her planned script.

"I got that part." He jerked his head toward the ring. "Rafe talk you out of it?"

"No." Darla frowned. "Did you want him to?"

He shrugged. "Only if you could be talked out of marrying me. I knew you wouldn't say yes to him. He's too wild and woolly for a straight-laced little mama like you."

She raised her brows. "You're not exactly tame yourself."

"But the difference is," Judah said, sitting on the bed to pull on his boots, "I'm willing to be tamed."

"I'm pretty sure every single woman in this town has set her cap for you at one time or another," Darla said, "and you've never been available for more than a one-night stand. Two nights at the most, according to gossip."

Judah grinned. "I wouldn't pay attention to gossip, darlin'. This town loves to talk, but talk's cheap."

"It may be cheap," Darla said, "but it's usually pretty much on the money."

He laughed. "Let's just say I'm trying to mend my ways, then."

"Anyway," Darla said, "let's go back to being the way we were before we ever...you know. Next time I talk to you—"

"I'll be a father?" He winked. "I think you're going about this all wrong, sweetheart."

"What do you mean?"

He leaned back, lounging on the bed. "This Dear John business. It's premature."

She edged toward the door, not trusting the look in his eyes, which had turned distinctly predatory. "How so?"

"Usually a Dear John letter is reserved for people who are breaking up, which implies that there was a relationship of some sort. We have no relationship. I would suggest, therefore, that you don't know what you're missing out on."

She blinked, trying to follow his thought process. "What exactly *am* I missing out on?"

He moved off the bed and took her in his arms. "Let me show you what you're trying to write off, babe."

She could feel warmth, and strength, and full-on sex appeal radiating from him. It made her weak in the knees, faint in the heart. The problem was, she'd always been in love with this man. She couldn't remember a time she'd ever wanted someone else. He ran his hands along her forearms up to her shoulders and she froze, mesmerized by his touch. She had no wish to escape him; she'd wanted to be in his arms for too many years. "This isn't a good idea."

"We don't know that it's a bad idea, either."

He kissed her on the lips, and she melted into his embrace. It hadn't been a dream; she hadn't imagined the overwhelming passion that swept her when he held her. At some point, she wondered why she was bothering to fight him when she wanted to be with him so much.

It was something about pride, she reminded herself, and not wanting to trap him. But it felt as if he was trying to entice *her* into a trap. "Judah," she said, breaking away from his kiss, "parenthood isn't a good reason to marry."

"It's not the worst reason. Ships have been launched because of babies, fiefdoms have risen and fallen. I say you let me kiss you for a while before we try to solve the world's big questions. Let's just figure out if you even like kissing me before you Dear John me." He slipped his hands along her waist, holding her against him. "You'd hate to kick yourself later for giving away a very good thing."

He was so darn confident that he held all the keys to her heart. Darla supposed he was like this with every woman. "Maybe the only way to prove that you're not as irresistible as you think you are is to prove you wrong."

"I'll take that dare," Judah said. "What time do you have to open the shop?"

She looked at him, her blood racing. "What difference does that make? You just kissed me, and I can live without it," she fibbed outrageously. "There's nothing between us that neither of us can't live without."

"I never said that," Judah said, "and you need to stop thinking so hard, my jittery little bride. I haven't even begun to kiss you."

Two hours later, Darla opened her eyes. "Oh, no!" she exclaimed, trying to leap from the bed, where Judah had seduced her until she was nothing but a boneless mush of crazy-for-him. He lay entangled with her so that she couldn't free herself from him, possessive even in sleep. He'd made her gasp with pleasure, cry out with delight, and then the man slept practically on top of her, assuring himself that she wouldn't get away without him knowing. She tried to move his big arms and legs off her, and he opened sleepy eyes, grinning at her.

"Move, Judah," she said, pushing at him. "I'm late to open the store!"

"Bad girl," he said, running a lazy hand over her hip. "Have the customers been waiting long?" he asked, kissing her shoulder.

"An hour." She felt his sneaky hand caress her backside, slip a finger inside her. She pushed at him with a little less enthusiasm, and he licked at one of her nipples, teasing it into instant hardness.

"Ready to tear up that Dear John letter yet?" he murmured.

"No," she said with determination. "Just because we had sex does not mean we're right for each other, Judah."

"Hmm," he murmured. "Clearly I have more convincing to do. The customers will have to wait while I plead my case."

He pressed her into the sheets, kissing her, torturing her with sexy passion, giving her no room for thinking of anything but him. Darla felt herself giving in once again. He knew exactly what he was doing to her.

The problem was, she didn't know if she worked the same magic on him.

"WHAT IF THERE'S NO SUCH thing as forever?" Darla asked Jackie that afternoon. "What if forever is just smoke and mirrors?"

Jackie glanced at her as she put away hand-beaded garters. "If you're talking about being audited, I'd say forever would be a real pain and I would hate it. I'd break the mirror and blow the smoke away."

Darla wrinkled her nose. "Forever as in marriage."

"Sometimes you have to throw caution to the wind. We sell the prepackaging to the dream here." Jackie waved a hand around the room. "We never thought we'd be so successful when we were planning this little adventure. We said, 'let's give it a shot and see how dumb we are to give up a good job, and try to sell dreams in a bad economy.'"

Darla nodded. "We did jump off a cliff without knowing what was beneath us."

Jackie nodded. "Marriage is the same thing."

Darla stared at her. "Does Pete know you feel like this? That you just took a leap of faith?"

"He took a leap of faith, too. I think it's harder for guys." Jackie giggled. "They don't know if we're going to decorate with lace doilies and leopard-skin rugs. They don't know if we're going to cook for them, or if we can. When Pete married me, he knew little about my cooking and less about how I might decorate. And then there's the biggest question of all."

Darla's eyes went wide. "Do men have all these deep thoughts? Or do they just dive in and hope it goes well?" Judah was probably a "diver." He didn't seem interested in her cooking or decorating. "What's the super-question?"

"Whether we're going to give them a lot of sex after marriage, or if we're just trying to drag them to the altar with lassos of lust."

Darla blinked. "They worry about that?"

Jackie shrugged. "It's a fact that there's a lot more nookie going on in the beginning than later. But that could be for any number of reasons, not necessarily lack of enthusiasm on the female's part."

"Have you been reading these bride magazines?" Darla sank onto a cabbage rose-printed sofa. "I don't think Judah worries too much about lovemaking."

"Because he's in romance mode right now. But on a subconscious level, he's figured out whether he wants to make love to you all the time, and if you'd like it. They like enthusiasm, too."

"Gee," Darla said, "all I was worried about was whether there was such a thing as forever."

"You're thinking romantically. Guys think logically. With their need barometer." Jackie giggled. "The comforts of hearth, home, kitchen, bed."

Darla liked being in bed with Judah—too much, if anything. "But there has to be more."

"Not for men. They don't get caught up in the fairy tale. It's pretty cut-and-dried."

"It doesn't sound very romantic."

"A moment ago you were wondering if forever was practical. It's not an illusion if both people have the same goals." Jackie laid some white gloves in the case. "Have you ever listened to the brides who come in here? They never talk about how wonderful their guys are. They talk about the dress, the flowers, the cake. Nothing that lasts."

"That's true," Darla said.

"They're in love with the icing," Jackie said, "when they should be focused on the cake."

"I don't remember you being so focused," Darla said. "When did this happen?"

"After I let Pete sweep me off my feet." She smiled. "You should let Judah sweep you. Trust me, it's a whole lot of fun to be romanced by your man."

Jackie and Pete had gotten married after Jackie had a surprise pregnancy. Pete appeared to be gaga over his bride—still.

"Even with three newborns, the romance is—"

"Hotter than a pistol." Jackie closed the cabinet. "I wouldn't worry about forever so much, Darla. I'd be enjoying my nights, if I was you. And coming in late every once in a while is a good thing, too. I can cover opening the store."

Darla blushed, wondering if Jackie knew that she hadn't been late because she'd overslept. Darla never overslept. "I can't think about anything else when he makes love to me," she admitted. "I'm holding out to see if we have anything in common that's not physical, but I'm not sure I'm going to be any good at telling him no. I gave Sabrina the magic wedding dress back, and then I found myself in bed with Judah. And it was wonderful."

"You *are* running in place, aren't you?"

Darla blinked. "You're right. I need a new plan."

Chapter Eleven

Darla called Judah that night and told him she was rescinding her offer of a marriage of convenience.

"Good," Judah said. "I'll be right over."

He hung up. Darla stared at the phone for a moment before racing to brush her hair. She should have anticipated him jumping the gun! She'd meant to tell him that she'd decided that they should wait to get married until after the children were born, when they'd had time to get to know each other better—and naturally, he'd drawn the conclusion he preferred.

Which was pretty much how it always was with Judah.

When she opened the door to him, she redoubled her vow to stick to the plan: no-nonsense laying out of the rules. It wouldn't be easy with him looking like a dark renegade cowboy ready to ravish her at any moment. She hadn't changed out of the comfy, dark gray sweat bottoms and pink polka-dotted halter maternity top, and still he looked at her as if she were edible.

"Tonight we lay everything on the table," Darla said.

"I'm all about tables," Judah said, "and I'm glad you're loosening up a bit. Let me show you what tables are best for, love."

And then to her shock, and beyond her wildest imaginings, Judah made love to her on the beautiful antique dining table where she usually laid out holiday dinners. "I'm afraid I'm too heavy for you," she whispered as he carefully placed her over him. He said, "No, baby. You're just right." And it was completely all right.

She felt like a million dollars as she collapsed with delicious shivers in Judah's arms.

"NO MORE OF THAT," Darla said, after the storm of lovemaking had abated. "We have to talk." She picked up her panties from the floor, collected her sweatpants from a chair and her halter top from the fruit bowl. Her sweats had been far too easy for Judah to take off—*she'd* been too easy. Far too much so.

He grinned. "I know talking is important, but I've always preferred action. I speak better with my hands."

She backed away from his dark appeal. "It doesn't surprise me that you would say that."

"Anyway," he said, "I can't really talk on an empty stomach. Can what you have to say wait until we eat?"

"Eat? At eight o'clock at night?"

He grinned. "Yeah. If this is a girlie chat, you really want me to have a full stomach."

"Girlie chat?" Outraged, she said, "First, just because you're near a table, Judah, doesn't mean all your needs have to be satisfied. Second—"

He kissed her to interrupt her, and pulled her close as he leaned back against the table. "Now, listen, missus, when you *are* my missus, I'll expect you in nothing but an apron, until my children are old enough to know that their mom is a dedicated nudie. Once the kiddos are off to college, you can return to cooking for me in the buff." Kissing her neck, he massaged her bottom, holding her tightly against him. "Questions?"

When she tried to open her mouth to give him the scolding of his life, he kissed her until she was breathless. He sighed, enjoying her quivering with rage. "Your limo driver will be here in about ten minutes. My guess is you'll want to change."

Darla's ire was drowned out by curiosity. "Limo driver?"

Judah released her, waving a negligent hand. "Or coachman. Whatever you romantic gals prefer to call them. I think they were called coachmen in the fairy tale, but they were mice first, and I thought ladies didn't like rodents and things. However, we will be attended by a first-rate rodent tonight."

Darla stared at Judah, wondering what kind of loose cannon had fathered her children. "What in the world are you talking about?"

The doorbell rang, and Judah bowed. "Better get your gown on, Cinderella. It's time for the ball."

"Ball?"

"Our date." Judah grinned. "Every woman wants to be swept off her little glass slippers, doesn't she? Though again, you'll have to forgive the rodent who's driving us." He flung open her front door. "She's not quite ready, bro," he said to Rafe, who walked in wearing some kind of chauffeur's uniform, or maybe a pilot's. Darla wondered what was going on. Rafe had proposed to her in sort of a bee-in-Judah's-eye way not twenty-four hours ago—why was he here now?

"Women are slow to get ready," Judah told Rafe. "And this one wanted to talk first," he said in a loud whisper to his brother.

Darla's gaze jumped to Judah, assessing whether he was trying hard to be a jackass, or if it just came naturally.

She decided it was the most natural thing in the world to him.

Rafe tipped his hat. "Can you hurry it up a bit, Darla? You look lovely the way you are, but I booked a flight plan, and there's a certain window of opportunity I should probably follow."

"Shh," Judah said, "don't give her too many details. She

argues when she has detail overload." He went over and kissed Darla. "Hurry, darling, the rodent gets nervous around midnight. He has a phobia about leaving on time."

She opened her mouth to argue, but Judah had claimed she liked to argue, so she really had no choice except to go into her room to examine her options.

There weren't many, she decided, as she tossed off the sweats and took a quick rinse. She wanted to talk, and Judah had left the door open for that. All he wanted to do was eat, he claimed, and though she had some organic veggies in the fridge, she sensed that wasn't what he had in mind. She slipped into a casual dress and tied her blonde hair up in a ponytail. Maybe this was his boneheaded way of being romantic. Judah probably didn't understand that a man didn't barge into a woman's house, ravish her on the dining room table and then announce he wanted to eat.

Yet it sounded romantic, as if Judah had put some thought into whatever his plan was. She slipped on some high heels—it would help her look him almost in the eye when she told him *no* the next time he tried to undress her. Had Rafe said something about a flight plan?

She went back into the den.

"Five minutes flat," Rafe said to Judah. "Dude, you can't do better than a girl who can beautify in five minutes."

Judah's gaze went from Darla's face to her dress, then slowly made its way up again. He grinned at her, and Darla knew instinctively he was thinking *dessert.*

She blushed. Or maybe *she'd* thought it.

"Come on," Rafe said, laughing. "There's so much electricity in this room there's going to be a fire."

Judah opened the door for her, and they left. She went to the Callahan family van, which was apparently serving as the limo tonight.

As soon as Rafe opened the door for her and Judah, she heard giggles and squeals.

"We're going to Chicago!" Sabrina exclaimed, and Darla saw that Jonas was in the back with her. "This is my sister, Seton," Sabrina said. "Seton, this is Darla Cameron, who is engaged to Judah." Sabrina smiled as Rafe took his place behind the wheel, next to her, completely missing the uncomfortable look on Darla's face. Judah slipped in next to Darla and whispered, "Are you okay with this?"

"Almost," she said. "Let me get over the shock."

He squeezed her shoulders gently. "I thought you might enjoy something fun."

No one else could hear Judah over the light jazz music softly playing and the excited chatter in the van, but Darla noted the kindness in his tone and realized he'd been acting like a rascal in her house just to bait her, knowing he had a romantic evening all planned, which delighted her. Dessert in Chicago would be so much fun.

And it was so much better than talking.

In fact, just about everything Judah wanted to do was better than talking. She sent a sidelong glance his way, enjoying him laughing as the girls teased him, and Rafe and Jonas ribbed him about being a worse date than he was a bull rider. And before long Darla felt herself falling for her man of action.

She'd fallen, she realized, completely under his spell.

It was too late to do anything but enjoy the ride.

"YOU SHOULDN'T HAVE LET her get away from you like that," Bode Jenkins said, over a gin and tonic that same evening. Sidney Tunstall shrugged his shoulders, not certain what difference it made to one of the wealthiest ranchers in these parts whether he got married or not.

It made a huge difference to Bode. He intended to make

certain the nuptials of Darla and Judah never happened. If there was one way to thwart Fiona—and he knew all about her little plan to grow her own zip code—it was to derail this wedding. "Your inheritance is all tied up in you getting married, and as the executor of your grandfather's estate, I have to make certain everything is proper." He gave Sidney a pensive look. "Who are you going to marry, since you've let Darla get away?"

Sidney shrugged. "I don't know."

"You have only another month before it all goes to charity." Bode shook his head. "It sure would be a shame to lose out on a couple million bucks."

Sidney shrugged again, not happy about the situation, but not fighting it, either. "That's just pocket change to some people, I guess. I lived without it before, and I can keep living without it."

Bode slammed a palm down on the mahogany table, one of the few nice furnishings he'd bothered to splurge on for his home. Julie had insisted on it. Lately, she'd been decorating a lot, despite his propensity to groan over the money spent. "You younger generation don't know what money is. I wouldn't let a penny get away from me, much less two million." Bode considered the man across from him. "You don't throw away a fortune, son."

"Under the parameters it was left to me, I can." Sidney straightened. "There's nothing wrong with waiting until I find the woman I love, Mr. Jenkins. And in a world where people now live to be a hundred, being a thirty-five-year-old bachelor isn't an emergency."

"Well, your grandfather thought you were dragging your feet. That's all I know." Bode shrugged, wondering how he could get the good doc to get off the dime and grab Darla away from that wild-eyed Callahan. Fiona's nephew had just stormed in there and thrown Sidney off the train, and apparently put stars of romance in Darla Cameron's eyes. He'd heard all about that from her mother, Mavis, who was the silliest, most cotton-headed woman he'd ever met. It was all love-this, and love-that, and Bode'd had it to the back teeth with all the Callahans and their ability to get everything they wanted. "If you liked Darla, why'd you surrender your ground, son?"

"Because I liked her," Sidney said, "I didn't love her. And she didn't love me."

"I see," Bode said thoughtfully. "You were going to take the money and run."

"No," Sidney said, showing a flash of temper, "I was going to take the money that was left to me, and be a husband to Darla and a father to her children. That's what the plan was."

"And you were never going to divorce?"

Sidney looked at him. "I suppose no one could ever say never, but I don't know why anybody would want to give up Darla. She's a nice lady."

Bode blinked, lit a cigar. "I do not understand your lack of competitiveness."

"I don't understand your thirst for it, so we're square." Sidney looked at Bode. "Is there anything else you need, Mr. Jenkins? I should probably be out looking for another wife, don't you think?" He said it sarcastically, and Bode caught that, but what he also caught was the *angle.*

"It will be hard to get another so quickly," Bode said, "one who has so much going for her. A man can find a woman anywhere, they're like fleas on a dog. But a good woman is tougher to find."

"Not exactly, Mr. Jenkins," Sidney said, getting his gentleman's ire up, which was just what Bode was hoping for. "They're nothing like fleas on a dog."

"Now, now, what I meant was that they are numerous, but not necessarily quality."

"I don't know what you meant, but it sounded pretty demeaning to me."

Bode laughed. "I never remarried after I lost my wife, Sidney. I think I know the value of a good woman."

Sidney looked at him, not appeased.

"Now, take my daughter, Julie—"

Sidney stood. "I'll find my own wife, Mr. Jenkins, if it's all the same to you."

Bode nodded. "Well, be quick about it. I'm very eager to write this check out to you instead of a charity. To be honest, I don't think much of charities, Sidney. I'm not certain that all that lovely money ever gets to the deserving folks who need it."

Sidney, white knight that he was, looked outraged. "There are many charities that do necessary, vital work."

"Yes, and it would be better in your pocket where you could decide on the charities of your choice. I'm not much for charity, as I said."

Sidney stared at him. "Are you trying to say that you decide where the money goes, if not to me?"

Bode pretended surprise. "Who else would?"

"My grandfather left no directive?"

Bode shook his head. "Nope. He figured you'd want the money badly enough to find your way to an altar, son. So maybe you ought to rethink letting Darla go, since the two of you had this nice little thing worked out."

Sidney sighed. "Tell me again how my grandfather came to choose you to be the executor of his estate?"

"Business, Sidney. We did business together. You might say we understood each other's world view, to a certain extent. And we went to school together, so we went back a long ways. He knew he could trust me."

Sidney looked at him a long time. "You're not trying to jump this will, are you, Mr. Jenkins?"

Bode grinned at him. "Sidney, from where you sit, two million dollars is a world of money. You can do a lot of good with it. You can have a nice house, send your kids to college. But for me, now, because I never let a penny go that had my name on it—unless Julie makes me—two million is good money, but it's not going to change my standard of life."

"I'm not sure you have a standard."

"That's where you're wrong." Bode smiled. "Your grandfather was a good man. And I always honor my friends."

Sidney put his hat on. "Thanks for the drink."

Bode nodded. "By the way, I have my doubts about Darla and Judah working out."

Sidney stopped. "What do you mean?"

"A little bird told me that they're planning to divorce as soon as the children are born. Now if you ask me," Bode said, his gaze sad, "that's a crying shame."

"I don't believe you."

"Ask Darla," Bode said, and Sidney said, "I will."

He closed the door.

Bode grinned and hummed a wedding march.

"IT WAS A LOVELY EVENING, Judah," Darla said at her front door when the "limo" returned her home. "Thank you."

"My pleasure," Judah said. "My truck's here, so I can leave, but of course, I can also stay if you want company."

Darla thought about the dining table and how she'd never be able to eat there again without remembering Judah loving her into a delirious frenzy. "It's been a long day. I have to be up early."

He nodded. "I understand."

She wondered if he understood something she wasn't necessarily saying. "Judah, why did you really plan the surprise trip tonight?"

He shrugged. "We haven't ever dated, for one thing, and

for another, I'm kind of hoping that tomorrow will be the day we get married."

A truck door slammed, and Sidney appeared.

"Hello, Darla," he said. "Judah."

She glanced at Judah, then at Sidney. "What are you doing here, Sidney?"

"Just feeling a bit wistful. Tomorrow's supposed to be our big day," he said. "Hope you don't mind me saying so, Callahan."

"Not at all," Judah said, "but I guess this is awkward. You two probably have things to discuss. Plans to end."

"Actually, I need to talk to both of you," Darla said.

Chapter Twelve

Darla seated her beaus on the sofa, gave them some tea, wondered if she should serve something stronger. They looked at her expectantly.

"Sidney," she began, "you and I were making a deal when we agreed to get married. That wasn't fair to you."

"I was okay with it," Sidney said. "I still need a wife. In a really bad way."

"There's a lot of women running around Diablo," Judah said helpfully. "Let me introduce you to some."

"I like this one," Sidney said, and Darla could tell he was baiting Judah.

"And Judah," she said, "there are some things between us that make me nervous. The condom prank, for one thing, which you never told me about. We shouldn't even be in this position." She took a deep breath. "I'm still in shock that I'm having twins."

"I'm a Callahan," Judah said. "Magic happens for us."

"Awkward," Sidney said. "And as a doctor, may I remind you that the female is responsible for some of the genetic coding?"

Judah shrugged. "But babies by the bunch are what we do at Rancho Diablo."

He said it in a *top that!* tone, and Darla sighed.

"Also," she said, "Sidney wasn't honest with you about your concussion."

Judah looked at Sidney. "Tunstall, you're a dirty dog. You made me think I'd cracked my nut. Did I even have a scratch?"

Sidney shrugged. "Perhaps there was something minor. Maybe." He sighed. "No. But I saved you from yourself. You needed to be here, with Darla, figuring out your future."

"You see," Judah said, "he's a gentleman, if not a good M.D."

Sidney shrugged again. "Whatever. I've had crankier patients."

"So," Darla said, interrupting their digging at each other, "this is my dilemma."

"No," Judah said. "You're having *my* children. There is no dilemma. We will find Sidney an appropriate bride of his own. I'll lend him my tux, but nothing else."

Sidney put his palms up in surrender. "I'm thinner than you, so the tux wouldn't fit. However, I can see that Darla has made up her mind—"

"I haven't made up my mind," Darla said quickly, feeling bad for Sidney, "because what I'm trying to tell both of you is that none of this started out right with either one of you."

"I don't care how it started out," Judah said. "I'm pretty happy with how things are proceeding. But if Sidney tries to marry the mother of my children, I'll give *him* a concussion he won't forget."

"He probably would." Sidney stood, went to the door. "He's a caveman, Darla. And I'm a gentleman. But ladies have always been attracted to bad boys. I know when I'm beat."

"That's right," Judah said, and Darla glowered at him.

"You're not beat, Sidney," she said softly, "but he is a caveman."

"I just took you to Chicago," Judah protested.

Sidney kissed Darla on the forehead. "You guys have a lot to work out. I'll shove off."

"Both of you shove off," Darla said in annoyance. "I think you two have a lot to work out."

"What?" Judah asked. "You can't expect us to be best friends. We're both too manly for that."

"It's hard competing for a woman," Sidney said. "So I'll have to agree with him."

"Both of you go," Darla said. "Now."

They looked at her, neither one happy.

"And don't come back until you've resolved your issues. I'm not having any hard feelings over a day that should be the happiest of my life."

"But—" Judah started, and Sidney said, "All right."

"Now, look here," Judah said, "this game of yours of always being Mr. Nice is tiresome. I can be nice, too."

Sidney shrugged. "If you own that emotion, own it. No one's standing in your way."

Judah frowned. "He's not going to fight fair," he complained to Darla. "I don't trust skinny bronc busters. He's already tried to put one over on me about my nonexistent concussion."

"That was your own fault," Sidney said righteously. "Even you should know if you bumped your head or not."

"I've had other things on my mind," Judah said with a growl Darla's way.

"Good night," she said, closing the door on both of them.

"What about tomorrow?" Judah called through the door.

"Tomorrow is another day," Darla told herself, and went to bed alone, already wishing Judah was there to hold her in his arms.

"WE'RE GOING TO HAVE TO be careful," Sidney said. "She might find another guy to marry."

"What are you talking about?" Judah wondered if the top

of his head was about to blow off. Was the doc crazy? In Judah's opinion, Darla loved no one but him—even if she hadn't realized it herself yet.

"If she has to choose between us," Sidney said reasonably, "she might opt for a third party."

They leaned against Judah's truck, chatting under the dark night sky as if discussing the stars. Judah grunted. "I'm not worried. I wouldn't let that happen."

"She's suffering with a guilt complex where you're concerned, so you might not have a say in the matter. Guilt doesn't make for an easy path to the altar."

Judah didn't care. "I'm getting her to the altar tomorrow. I have the rest of our lives to let her make up to me for all that guilt she's worried about."

"I don't know if that's the proper approach."

"You're my shrink now? My love doctor?"

"Someone's got to do it," Sidney said. "Look, I don't mind helping you, but I'm in a ditch. I need her, too. So don't push me."

"What's your deal?" Judah asked. "What's it going to take to get you convinced that Darla is not the bride you want? Because frankly, you're not going to have her."

"Remember I was first," Sidney said. "That flower arch in her backyard has my name on it, so to speak."

"What flower arch?" Judah's head turned like it was on a swivel. "I don't see an arch."

"Notice that all the little elves have been busy while you were chasing romance in Chicago."

In his haste to try to get past Darla's front door tonight, he hadn't noticed the lanterns strung along her porch, and candles wrapped with pink ribbons along the drive. "Okay, what's the plan? I'm open to suggestions right now. Because she returned the ring to me. And I heard she gave Sabrina some stupid magic wedding dress, not that I believe in magic."

Judah thought about the wild horses that ran across the far reaches of Rancho Diablo. They hadn't been seen in a while. Maybe good luck had left him behind. "I do believe in magic," he said after a moment, "and right now, I need some."

"Yeah, me, too." Sidney nodded. "I was sent here tonight to break you two up."

Judah didn't let himself show his surprise. "So you're the villain in my fairy tale."

"There's nothing Bode Jenkins would rather see more than you and Darla calling things off."

"Over my cold dead body will that happen."

Sidney nodded. "I thought so. Anyway, that's why I came over tonight. Hope I haven't confused matters between you and Darla."

"What do you mean?"

Sidney shrugged. "Just in case she's in there right now having second thoughts. Third thoughts."

"She's not."

"Bode's determined to get at your family. I should probably keep my mouth shut, considering he holds some of my purse strings at the moment, but he's playing foul."

"Look," Judah said, "I don't know how to help you with your problem. I wish I did. But don't let Bode talk you into a wedding you don't want."

"Yeah," Sidney said, almost reluctantly. "I don't want it. And Darla doesn't love me, either. She's always loved you."

"Not me," Judah said, and Sidney said, "Yes, you. You're the only one who doesn't know it."

Judah blinked, considered whether Sidney knew what he was talking about or was trying to dig himself out of a pounding courtesy of Judah's big fists. "Did Darla tell you that?"

Sidney got in his truck. "You'll have to find out on your own. I've done all the repairs on my conscience I intend to. I'll be here tomorrow, waiting to move in if you don't do the job properly, though. And if you don't mind, keep this conversation under your big hat. I don't want Bode deciding to claim my inheritance. You have a trustworthy aunt who oversaw your affairs. Bode is a different proposition altogether."

Judah tipped his hat. "Be here with your tux on," he said. "I need a best man, and you'll fit the bill just fine."

Sidney looked at him. "Are we inviting gossip?"

"Just letting everyone know that the bride's a smart lady. She's got good taste in men. And you can show Bode he doesn't own you."

"He does, in a way, but that's out of my control now." Sidney backed his truck up. "Let me know if you come across an extra bride."

"By chance have you ever met Diane, Aberdeen's sister? She's not exactly looking for marriage, but you might change her mind. Anyway, good luck." He waved, and when the doctor's truck had disappeared, he marched to Darla's bedroom window. He tapped and a moment later she appeared, looking none too pleased to see him.

"Judah! What are you doing?" she asked through the glass.

"Serenading you."

She slid the window open. "Go away."

"I can't. We have to talk."

"So talk."

"Let me in, Darla."

She shook her head. "Not a chance, buster."

"What is it?" he asked, his voice innocent. "What's got my bride thinking less than happy thoughts the night before her wedding?"

"I'm not getting married tomorrow," Darla said, "even though everyone is conspiring to make it happen."

"I got blood drawn. I'm ready to rock," Judah said. "It looks like the decorating is done, and you've got a dress. We can go get a marriage license in the morning, and be ready to say 'I do' at sundown."

She shook her head. "I'm not a girl who rushes in to things."

Judah put his hands on the window ledge and hauled himself into Darla's bedroom. "Whew, I'm getting too old for this," he said. "I hope you plan on being a more agreeable wife than you are a fiancée."

"I'm not your fiancée. And you're not supposed to be in here." Darla closed the window and pointed a finger toward the den. "Go out there if you want to talk."

"It's dangerous for you out there, too," Judah said. "I like variety."

She didn't reply, but he could tell she wasn't exactly rejecting his suit. "So back to this guilt thing," he said. "I don't care if Creed's stupid condoms failed. I'm going to have the most beautiful babies in the world. And I don't care about Doc trying to give me the shove. I like him. He's entitled to want the most beautiful woman in Diablo, too. So," Judah said, crossing to take her face between his hands, "can we put all this guilt business behind us? Because you really, really want to marry me, and frankly, putting me back out in the stream to be fished by other ladies is a move you'd always regret."

Darla closed her eyes, allowing herself to relax in his grasp. "Let's sleep on it. I'm too tired to think tonight."

"I've waited a long time to hear that. Come on, love, let me put you to bed."

He pulled Darla toward the bed, pressing her down into the sheets. He lay down next to her, tugging her up against him spoon-style, and rubbed her back until she fell asleep. Once she was breathing deeply and he could tell she was out like a light, he cupped a palm under her tummy—under his boys—and fell asleep himself, feeling like a million bucks.

Chapter Thirteen

Darla would have liked to pretend that she surrendered, but when she stood at the altar the next evening after a whirlwind of last-minute preparations, she knew she was marrying Judah because she'd always dreamed of it. Whatever they were letting themselves in for, he was going to be her husband, and she was going to be Mrs. Judah Callahan, exactly what she'd always wanted.

She wasn't strong enough to resist her dreams another day. She couldn't imagine not marrying him. In that, Judah was egotistically right: she didn't want to return him to the dating pond for other women to catch. She wanted him all to herself.

Maybe he wasn't the marrying kind, but she had to take a chance that he was.

Everyone was happy, smiling at the wedding. The evening was lovely, the air sweetened with romance. Judah was breathtakingly handsome and sexy; she couldn't believe he was actually going to be hers.

"Are you ready?" Jackie asked, coming to her side.

Darla nodded. "Thanks for being my maid of honor."

"I'm happy to have a sister." Jackie hugged her. "Judah's out there pacing. If we don't get you down the aisle, he's going to come get you."

Darla smiled. He'd been gone this morning when she'd

awakened, but he'd left a note on her pillow telling her that she was the luckiest woman in the world, and she'd always be the envy of every other woman in town.

Typical Judah.

"I'm ready," Darla said.

"Just a small warning," Jackie said, "so you won't be surprised. Bode's here."

"I didn't invite him." The news did nothing to calm her nerves.

"Bode is like the troll that no one ever invites, but he manages to hang around. I vote ignore him, and completely ruin his day. Fiona told him that if he did one thing to upset you, she'd have him tied to a cactus. And I won't tell you what Judah said about it."

Darla felt better. "Let's hurry before something bad happens. I distinctly feel an urge to speed this along."

Jackie waved to Diane, who was in charge of overseeing the music. Diane motioned for the harpist to begin, and serene music filtered through the air, joined by a traditional piano wedding march. Darla took a deep breath and headed down the aisle as Diane's little daughters scattered rose petals from white baskets along her path.

Judah was smiling at her, eating her up with his eyes as she walked to the beautiful altar. An excited tingle shot up her spine. This sexy man was about to tell the world that he was making her his wife. It was all her dreams come true.

A shot rang out, and in front of Darla's horrified eyes, Judah fell back against Sidney, who helped him to the ground. Guests cried out, scattering, and the wedding march ground to a halt. The little flower girls ran to Diane, and suddenly, Darla was grabbed by big strong Callahans and dragged away from the altar—and Judah. She protested, wanting to be at his side, but Sam held her back, keeping her out of danger.

Darla shrugged Sam off and ran to Judah's side. She could

hear Sidney calling for an ambulance as he worked to stop the bleeding in Judah's arm.

"Judah," she said, kneeling down next to him, despite the hands trying to pull her back, "don't you *dare* die on me!"

He gave her a weak smile. "I've been shot before. This is just a flesh wound. Don't get my babies all upset over nothing."

"How do you know it's a flesh wound? Sidney, is it a flesh wound?" She didn't wait for an answer. Her heart was painfully tight in her chest as she watched the blood oozing from him. "What do you mean, you've been shot before? You never told me that!"

"Hunting accident," he said. "Anyway, it wasn't important. We had a lot more important things to talk about."

"That's it," Darla said. "As soon as you're patched up, you're moving in with me. I'll make sure you stay out of trouble."

He closed his eyes, and Sheriff Cartwright's men surrounded the wedding party, moving everyone away in case the shooter was still out there. "Go," Judah told her, "I don't want you getting shot. Do what the nice lawmen tell you. Isn't that right, Doc?"

"That's right," Sidney said, and Darla said, "Shut up, both of you. I'm not going anywhere until I know you're not exaggerating about your flesh wound."

Sidney waved to the Callahan men, who were standing around helplessly. "Get him inside," he said, "not near windows, until the ambulance arrives."

But that wasn't necessary. The ambulance pulled up, its sirens wailing, and two EMTs jumped out to take over from Sidney, who looked gravely concerned.

"I know we've had our differences, but I hope you know I didn't do this," Sidney said.

"I know you didn't," Judah said.

Sidney watched protectively as Judah was placed into the ambulance. "I'm going to ride with him."

"I'm going, too." Darla shoved her way into the vehicle behind Sidney.

"All this stress isn't good for the babies," Sidney warned, and Judah said, "Stay here, Darla."

She shook her head. "My children would never forgive me if I didn't stay with their father when he'd been shot."

"More guilt," Judah said, and Darla said, "That's right. Now just lie there."

"I'm going to love being married," Judah said, his face creased with a smile even though he closed his eyes wearily.

"I'm hoping this wasn't your way of getting out of marrying me," Darla said, and Judah's eyes snapped open.

"Not a chance, sweetheart. Not a chance."

Darla looked at the blood on her wedding dress and wondered if she should have worn the magic wedding gown, after all. She'd definitely seen Judah standing behind her in the mirror. He'd been smiling, handsome, tall and virile. Not shot by a sniper. Gooseflesh jumped onto her arms, and she rubbed them, not able to rub away the unease as the ambulance raced to the hospital.

"YOU SEE WHAT I MEAN," Sabrina whispered to her sister, Seton. "There's a dark cloud over Rancho Diablo."

Seton nodded. "I've been keeping an eye on the Jenkins's place, but I have to be honest with you, I don't think the old man did it. He seemed shocked when Judah got hit. Not displeased, necessarily, just shocked."

Sabrina blinked. "Who else would have done it?"

"Maybe the best man set it up. Weren't they romantic rivals?"

"You'd have to get to know Sidney to understand that he wouldn't hurt anyone," Sabrina said. "The man is gentle. He's a healer." She could see that in his peaceful aura, in the kindness in his eyes. He'd never borne any ill will toward Judah, and she knew Judah liked the doc, too. "No, it wouldn't have been Sidney."

"Any other ideas?"

Sabrina shook her head. "The Callahans are well-liked in the town, as you might have been able to tell by the number of guests who showed up to the wedding. And that was for a wedding no one thought would actually happen."

"Well, it didn't." Seton glanced around Darla's property, watching the guests help clean up the yard and put away chairs. "The thing that puzzles me is that whoever shot Judah either wasn't a practiced assassin or didn't mean to kill him."

"Why? What are you thinking?"

Seton shrugged. "I think someone just wanted Judah—or the Callahans—to know he was out there. Scare them a little bit. Or, and the possibility is remote, it could have been a random misfire from a hunter. But I don't think so. It didn't sound like a large firearm."

Sabrina sighed. "Hold that thought. Bode and Fiona are having a row, and since I've been employed by both, I'd better see if I can run interference."

"I'm telling you," Bode said angrily to Sheriff Cartwright as Sabrina walked up, "I didn't have anything to do with the shooting. And she hit me! That's assault. And I want to know what you're going to do about it, Sheriff."

"Not much, Bode, and you're not, either." The sheriff rocked back on his heels. "Do you have an invitation to be here?"

Bode's mouth flattened. "One doesn't need an invitation to attend a wedding of a local favorite. It was known by all that a wedding would take place here today."

Fiona looked at him. "Bode, one day, things are going to turn out badly between you and me. I suggest you keep your dealings with my family on the professional level, and quit being such a pest."

Bode didn't reply and Fiona left, with Sabrina following her. "Fiona, let me drive you to the hospital. We'll check on Judah and Darla."

Fiona nodded. "I'd appreciate that. They don't need me at the hospital, I'm sure, but if I stay here, I'm going to have more fighting words with that scoundrel."

"We don't want that." Sabrina steered Fiona toward the van, waved at Burke so he'd know they were leaving, in case he wanted to ride along. He did, and so did Seton, which made Sabrina feel better, having her sister around. Diane said, "I'll hold down the fort," and Fiona shouted, "Thanks!" out the window, and off they went to see how Judah was surviving his big day that hadn't turned out the way anybody had hoped.

"I'M FINE," Judah said for the hundredth time, thinking that having a nurse for a fiancée had its blessings and its curses. Darla hovered over the nurses, she hovered over the doctors, she hovered over Judah. No one escaped her watchful eye. He reminded himself that this was one of the things he'd known about her, that she was efficient and businesslike.

But he was a man, and he didn't want to be fussed over. Not about a gunshot wound, anyway. The truth was, dark thoughts kept running through his mind, torturing him, and he wanted to reflect on them.

What if the bullet had hit Darla?

What if his babies had been injured?

His blood ran cold, keeping him shivering, as the worries punctuated his blood loss.

"If you're cold, I'll get a heated blanket," Darla said, and a small redheaded nurse said, "I'll get it," anxious to stay out of Darla's path. She was as protective of him as a lioness, and

Judah closed his eyes, not wanting to think about how much he wanted to marry her.

He was glad now that he hadn't.

"Darla," he said, as they began to wheel him toward an operating room, "today was not our day."

Tears jumped into her eyes. He hated to see her cry. If he had his way, a tear would never form on his behalf in her eyes, ever again.

"We'll have another day," Darla said. "We'll work something out."

He gave her a small grimace of a smile before he was wheeled to the O.R. so the bullet could be removed. He didn't care about the bullet. He cared about what had been taken from them today, which was romance and innocence.

It made him angry. Worse, the shooting had given him crystal-clear perspective. Until today, he hadn't really thought through what he was doing to Darla by marrying her.

But now he remembered. And now he knew what he had to do.

Chapter Fourteen

Sam waited until Bode walked up the drive of the Jenkins place before he launched himself at him, landing on top of the elderly man. Bode cursed, trying to throw a punch, but Rafe caught his hand.

"Mind your manners, Jenkins." Rafe held him down and Sam took a seat on the man's back.

"*My* manners?" Bode spit some dirt out of his mouth. "I'll have the law on you so fast it'll made your head spin if you don't get your ape of a brother off me. You Callahans have never been anything but trouble, you and your crazy aunt, too."

"Crazy!" Sam said. "Brother, did you just hear him insult our aunt, who raised us when no one else would have?" He leaned over from his seated position on Bode's back to look him in his eyes. "Bode, we're curious just how far back your animosity goes."

"It goes back years. Why the hell wouldn't it?" Bode demanded. "If you need a carbon dating, you could probably date it to the time your parents arrived here."

"We wonder what really happened to our parents," Rafe said as Jonas walked out of the neatly manicured bushes around Bode's property.

"There's no one here and Julie doesn't appear to be home,"

Jonas said to his brothers. "You're free to conduct yourselves as you see fit."

"And you call yourself a lawyer," Bode snarled in Sam's direction. "Get off of me, you hooligan. All of you are insane, like your silly aunt."

"Ah," Rafe said with a sigh, "I'm just dying to hit him."

"But we won't," Sam said, "because that would be against the law. We're just having a chat with our neighbor." He bounced on Bode's back, drawing another snarl.

"I don't know what happened to your parents," Bode said. "That I swear."

"Your word's not really good with us," Jonas said, "if you don't mind me pointing out the obvious."

"What do you think I would have done with them? And if you really want to know, why don't you ask Fiona?" Bode tried to get up, but Sam was too heavy to be budged. He patted Bode on the head, comforting him like a child, and the old rancher cursed at him.

"Someone shot Judah tonight, and no one would do that but you. You're too clever to get caught," Jonas said, "so you hired some punk to do it. Luckily for you, Judah isn't dead, or you'd be joining him in pushing up daisies."

"Why would I want to kill your brother? Why don't you suspect the man he stole Darla from?" Bode demanded.

"That's too easy," Sam said. "First of all, Doc wouldn't hurt anybody. Second, you want us gone, scared off. When the ballistics on the bullet come back, we're going to have Sheriff Cartwright search your house for a match, and any records for a weapon that's been sold to you, licensed to you, ever fired by you at a tin can."

"I didn't do it. I really don't want any of you boys to come to harm. I swear it."

Sam bounced on Bode's back a little harder, and the rancher *oofed* into the dirt. "You say that now, while we've got you cornered. But we know you sneaked into our house and locked Pete in the basement. You threaten us constantly, and our aunt. So we know to come to you when we so much as find a piece of bread missing from the pantry."

Bode shook his head. "I'm not talking any more until I have a lawyer and the sheriff here."

"Why? We're not arresting you, Bode. We're just asking a few friendly questions. The truth is, we want to save you from yourself," Rafe said.

"How so?"

"Because you really don't want to be the jackass that you are," Jonas said. "We know deep inside you beats a heart that doesn't want to harm anyone. Isn't that right, Bode?"

"I want your land," Bode said. "And that's it. But I can figure out a hundred ways to get it besides killing people. I'm too smart for that."

Sam glanced around at his brothers, then got off Bode and rolled him with his boot so that he faced three angry Callahans.

"Bode," Jonas said, "just so you know, we'll do whatever it takes to keep you from owning one inch of our land."

"It's too late," Bode said, the corners of his mouth lifting with glee. "Your aunt is broke. She has no money. She made bad investments, and it's only a matter of time before I put all of you out on the road with nothing but your belongings. And I look forward to that day, boys. Your aunt and Burke, too, and all those hobos you take in."

Jonas sighed. "Pride goeth before a big-ass fall, Jenkins. Just remember I told you that."

"Maybe," Bode said, "but some of us don't fall."

"We'll see," Sam said, and the brothers walked away.

"THERE'S GOING TO BE WAR on the ranch," Fiona said to her friends as they sat in the back room of the Books'n'Bingo shop. "It may not be quite full-blown war, but I'm really afraid it's coming."

Mavis stared at her. "How can we help you?"

"I need help plotting more than anything else. There's got to be a way to think myself out of the box I'm in." She sipped her tea, and glanced around at the faces of her three best friends. These women had been with her through thick and thin from the day she'd arrived in New Mexico. Their friendship had strengthened and sustained her over the years at Rancho Diablo. Now she needed it more than ever. "The worst part is that the wedding had to called off. I'm so sorry about Darla's big day," she told Mavis.

"I'm confused," Corinne Abernathy said. "First I ordered a tea set for a wedding gift to give Darla and Dr. Tunstall, and then I had to change the card to make it to Darla and Judah, and now I don't know what to do!" Corinne blinked. "I think I'll take it back to the store. It's not a lucky tea set, for certain."

"I suppose you could give it to one of your nieces," Nadine Waters suggested. "Seton or Sabrina might like it."

"Don't worry," Mavis said. "Darla might be my late-in-life child, but she's always quick to resolve her dilemmas. And that tea set is lucky, I'm certain, Corinne." She patted her friend's hand.

Fiona sighed. "This is all my fault."

"There is no fault." Mavis shook her head. "It's just that Bode Jenkins can't leave well enough alone."

"I beaned him pretty good with my purse at the wedding. And it had Burke's pocket watch in it, too, which as you know is no light thing. I heard it go thump on Bode's thick skull."

"Why were you carrying Burke's watch?" Corinne asked.

"Sabrina had taken it somewhere to get it cleaned a couple months ago. She knew of a person who specializes in antique pocket watches. Burke does so love his timepiece," Fiona said with a sigh. "That watch has been running for over half a century now."

"Like you," Corinne said with a giggle.

"That's true," Mavis said. "Hope you didn't mess up the watch by using it as a nunchuku."

Fiona shook her head. "The watch has a gold case. It's like a rock, a lucky Irish rock." She looked around the sitting room of the Books'n'Bingo shop, taking in all the volumes of beloved books, the various teapots lining the walls for decoration and for use, and sighed at the coziness of it all. "I just wish everything would settle down for just a little while. Mostly, I want Darla and Judah to get married. I want you to be my in-law," she told Mavis. "Even though you're all my sisters, I was really looking forward to adding one of you to my family tree. And I do so love Darla. She's just always so nice to me. Everybody in our family likes her so much."

Mavis blinked. "To be honest, as much as I think Sidney is a great doctor, I was really pulling for Judah. I think those two have been making secret cow eyes at each other for years."

Corinne nodded. "At least you'll be getting more grandchildren, Fiona. That's more than I can say for myself. Goodness knows neither Seton nor Sabrina are interested in being altar-bound."

Fiona contemplated that over a sugar cookie. "I was just positive it was a stroke of brilliance for me to hire Sabrina to light a fire under my boys, since they have no idea you have nieces, Corinne. The fortune teller bit was priceless. And it's a bonus that Seton is a private investigator, because now I can spy on Bode to my heart's content."

"But none of it's working," Nadine said. "Bode's still being ugly, and only two of your boys jumped at the chance to own the ranch. I mean, I think Judah will still make an excellent groom, Mavis," she hurriedly said, "when he gets over being shot."

"Being shot does slow a groom down." Fiona threw out that last bit to comfort Mavis, but the truth was, she feared that a wedding postponed might be a wedding canceled for good. "I'm all for striking while the bride is hot, though."

Mavis gasped. "Darla will always be hot! There are good genes in our family!"

"I meant iron," Fiona soothed. "You know Darla is a silver-blond beauty, Mavis. Don't get in a twist. I'm just so nervous and rattled my mouth is running off like a rabbit." She did feel completely rattled, and it wasn't fair. She didn't like not being in control. "I've always pushed my boys to do what I believed was best for them, and I want Judah right back at the altar before Bode figures out a way to…to—"

She couldn't bring herself to think about the fact that Bode had tried to kill her nephew. "You know, they said the bullet was small, not meant to do anything more than incapacitate, but I don't believe that. Even a .22 can kill."

"Shoot, even a BB gun can kill a person," Nadine said morosely. "My husband used to shoot varmints with BBs, and you'd be surprised the damage they can do."

"I don't want to think about it," Fiona said, swallowing against a rush of coldness seeping into her body. What would her brother, Jeremiah, and Molly say if she let something happen to one of their sons? She had to keep the family whole and together—and at Rancho Diablo. "Judah will go home from the hospital tomorrow, and then we'll see what he's planning."

"I hope he's planning another wedding," Nadine said, and Fiona nodded.

"Me, too. I've about run out of lures to convince these boys that marriage is the holy grail." Fiona put down her teacup and pursed her lips for a moment. If Bode had gone to the trouble of harming Judah, basically scaring him away from Darla, then her plan of getting the boys married off was working.

She just didn't know why. "Why wouldn't Bode want Judah to marry Darla?"

"Because your family is growing and his is not, and he's a jealous old coot," Corinne said with some heat. "You don't think he'll ever allow his daughter, Judge Julie, to leave his house, do you? So while you've got grandkids popping out all over, he has no hopes whatsoever of having any at all. Because he'll never allow Julie to leave his home to marry someone. And pity the poor man who ever does try to take her off Bode's hands."

Fiona snapped her fingers. "That's what we need to do."

"What?" Nadine asked, lost. "What are we doing?"

"If we find a beau to hang around Bode's, eager-beaver for Julie, Bode won't have time to be in my business!" Fiona said with delight. "I believe the shock would almost end his ability to do harm to anyone on the planet."

"Except for the poor suitor," Nadine said. "You couldn't pay a man to date poor Julie."

Fiona blinked. "There's that."

Corinne nodded. "For every plot, there's a twist."

"But maybe the best way to declare war," Fiona said, "is to take it right to his door."

"We don't know a bachelor brave enough nor stupid enough to… Why are you looking like that?" Nadine asked. "Fiona, it appears as if someone turned a lightbulb on over your head."

Fiona smiled. "I have three nephews left, and all of them are very brave, and not stupid in the least."

Her friends stared at her.

"Can you imagine how upset Bode would be if one of my nephews started coming around his place? He wouldn't be able to focus on anything but Julie, and we could plan another wedding!" Fiona clapped her hands. "I just knew we'd come up with an answer if we brainstormed enough!"

"It could work," Corinne said. "In fact, it's impressive. I do see one tiny problem, however."

They all looked at her expectantly. Corinne shrugged. "Which one of your nephews would you sacrifice to the dragon, Fiona?" Just as she posed the question, the store bell tinkled and Darla walked in, locking the door behind her.

"Darla!" Mavis exclaimed. "What are you doing here?"

Darla accepted a cup of tea from Fiona and took a tufted chair in the circle. "This is the only place where I can come and have a good...I don't know. I don't want to cry, but I definitely want to talk to women who've been through everything."

The four women looked at her carefully, and Darla felt comforted by their interested perusal. If anyone could give her solid advice, it was these four.

She hoped they had some advice.

"Are you feeling all right?" Corinne asked.

"The babies are okay?" Nadine inquired.

"Did you just come from the hospital?" Fiona demanded.

"Yes, yes and yes," Darla said. "Judah is raising Cain with the doctors to release him, so he's in peak form."

"As I expected." Fiona nodded with satisfaction. "All the Callahans are tough nuts."

Darla nodded in turn. "Tougher than you think. Judah broke off our engagement."

"What?" The women exclaimed as one and began offering sympathy in huge doses, which Darla needed.

"That scoundrel," Fiona said. "Honey, he didn't mean a word of it. You just give him a day or two to cool off, and he'll be throwing himself at your feet again, if I know my nephew."

Darla's heart was heavy as she shook her head. "I don't think so this time. He said there are too many things that endanger me and the children for him to marry me. He said there are too many family ghosts, and until they're laid to rest, he can't put me in jeopardy."

"With two little babies on the way he doesn't want to marry you?" Mavis asked, proud mother coming to the fore. "Fiona, I don't think your nephew is being honorable."

Fiona puffed up like a small bird. "If there's one thing Judah is, it's honorable, Mavis Cameron Night." She leaned toward Darla. "It sounds like shock to me, Darla. We have no family ghosts, not really, not of the variety that would harm anyone, anyway."

Everyone stared at Fiona. Darla said, "I'm not afraid of ghosts. He is."

"Silliest thing I ever heard," Nadine said. "Ghosts at a wedding, indeed. Fiona, you tell Judah to buck up."

Darla's heart hung heavy in her chest. After all of Judah's romancing her through her own case of cold feet, she had never expected to hear him say that the wedding was off.

He felt that she was safer without him.

It broke her heart.

Fiona looked uncomfortable. "I think there's been a miscommunication."

Darla shook her head. "After the surgery, he distinctly said, 'I can't marry you, Darla—'"

"Pain pills," Nadine sniffed. "Sounds like they fed him a handful, and I wouldn't listen to a word he said, Darla. You were a nurse. You know how drugs can make people time travel right out of their normal dispositions. I've never seen a man crazier for a woman than Judah is for you."

"He said it's not safe," Darla said, not drawing any comfort from their words. "He said that in order to keep me safe, he has to keep away from me."

"I don't understand," Fiona said, blinking. "It's like he got shot with the opposite of Cupid's arrow."

"Yeah, it was called Bode's bullet," Mavis said.

"Oh, dear," Fiona said. "Darla, I'm so very sorry. Surely this will all pass after my renegade nephew gets out of the hospital. He was never very good with injuries, you know that. Look at the last one he had. He thought he had a concussion when he didn't. I'm not saying Judah's a wienie, but he's not a patient patient, and—"

"It's all right," Darla said, even though it wasn't. Her heart was shattered.

"Well, it just shows you should have married Dr. Tunstall," Mavis said hotly. "Dr. Tunstall wouldn't have put you through all this nonsense. He's a steady man with a good income, and no one would shoot at *him.*"

Fiona stiffened. "That's my nephew you're calling unsteady, Mavis."

"That same nephew who can't be bothered to read a big-ass label that says Party Condoms on the side," Mavis returned, her cheeks pink.

"Prank Condoms," Darla said. "And it was just as much my fault as is. I seduced him."

The women went quiet, staring at her.

"I did," Darla said. "I've been wanting to for years, and I'd do it again in a heartbeat. In fact, I'd seduce him tonight if he didn't have an injury. But it really doesn't matter. Judah has vowed to stay five miles away from me until all the ghosts in your family have been laid to rest. That's what he said, and I could tell he meant every word."

"What are these ghosts, Fiona?" Corinne asked. "I don't remember anything phantasmagoric hanging about your place."

Fiona cleared her throat. "I think Judah means the whole Bode problem."

Darla shook her head. "He muttered something about aunts who keep secrets."

"Well," Fiona said uncomfortably, at her friends' curious perusal. "Pain pills are powerful."

Mavis gathered her teacup and purse. "You'd best talk to your nephew, Fiona. We have another suitor in the wings, and we're not going to wait around for Judah. To be frank, it sounds like the man got a case of winter-cold feet. Darla shouldn't be dumped and humiliated—"

"Mom," Darla said, "I'm not humiliated."

"You will be when your children are born and people wonder why you and Judah were getting married and then didn't." Mavis glared at Fiona. "This is what happens when you meddle, Fiona. Clearly, you hurried a man along who wasn't ready to accept his responsibilities. Getting shot is no excuse. Darla's a nurse, for heaven's sake. If anybody could nurse a man back to health, it's her."

"Oh, dear," Nadine said. "We need more tea. And cupcakes."

"Ladies," Corinne said, "I vote we adjourn our chat before fur really begins to fly, and words are spoken that can never be taken back."

"Goodness," Fiona said, "this is all a tempest in a teapot."

"A cracked pot, if you ask me. Come on, Darla," Mavis said, and swept from the store.

Darla blinked, then hugged Fiona goodbye. "It's not your fault," she whispered. "I always knew he didn't really love me. Not the way I was in love with him."

Darla followed her mother. "Mom, you shouldn't have said those things to poor Fiona. It's not her fault someone shot Judah."

"She raised a back-sliding nephew," Mavis said, "and it's high time she get her house in order over there."

Darla sighed. There was a house that needed to be put in order, and it was her own. Her mother wouldn't want to hear that right now—she was too upset over everything that had happened, and Darla understood. Everyone was upset. People would be talking in Diablo for weeks.

But she didn't care. All Darla knew was that Judah had pursued her, finally convincing her that she was the only woman for him. Even if it had been all about the babies, he'd still pursued her.

Now she intended to pursue him. She owed it to her children, and to their father, to make certain that they all ended up as a happy family, no matter how many ghosts Judah thought he had to protect her from.

She was in love with him, and he was just going to have to deal with that. *And I've never been afraid of ghosts, or anything else that goes bump in the night. What I fear is losing the one man I know in my heart is a good man, the right man, the only man, for me.*

Chapter Fifteen

The next evening Fiona walked into the bunkhouse and gave her four nephews, who were trying to resurrect their lagging game of Scrabble, a baleful stare. "Judge Julie's got herself quite the conundrum," she said. "She's trying to get that longhorn you brought from El Paso untangled from the fence, and she's wearing a tight dress and fishnets. I guess that's what a beautiful judge wears under her black robes." Fiona bleated a pitiful sigh—theatrical, to Judah's ears—and said, "I never knew why you boys had to have that longhorn, but if I was you, I'd go save it from the judge. Julie looks fit to slip it on the grill."

Jonas, Rafe and Sam abandoned Judah on the double, as Judah was certain Fiona had hoped they would. She looked at her nephew. "Why aren't you at the main house?"

"I'm fine here," Judah said.

"Usually when you boys have some kind of issue, you stay at the house."

"I don't have an issue," Judah said, not about to be lured by coddling.

She put her hands on her hips, staring at his arm, which he'd propped on a pillow. He preferred that to wearing the sling the doctor had given him. The sling made him feel like an invalid, and Judah wasn't giving in to any weaknesses when he most needed to be strong.

"You do have issues," Fiona said. "What in the world did you mean by telling Darla about ghosts?"

Judah shook his head, in no mood to be questioned the day after his wedding had taken a sinister turn. He leveled a wary eye on his aunt. "You should know about ghosts, Aunt."

"Well, I don't. I've never seen a ghost in my life," she snapped, and he grunted at her truculent tone.

"I don't know what all you've been keeping to yourself, Aunt Fiona. All I know is that Darla might have taken a bullet that was meant for me. And until I've got everything figured out, I'm not putting her in harm's way."

"The only harm that's going to come is when she decides not to wait for your silly butt." His aunt glared at him. "You do not take a bullet and then use that as an excuse, a pitiful one, not to marry the best woman that's ever been placed in your path. Trust me, even a woman who owns a shop full of wedding regalia doesn't put on the old satin-and-lace lightly. You should rethink your situation when you're not chock-full of hallucinogens."

"I haven't taken any pills," Judah said. "I don't like pain pills. So don't worry."

"You're not thinking straight, and I hate to see you make the mistake of a lifetime. You're going to look quite the ass when Darla marries Sidney."

"She won't," Judah said, though he didn't admit to a twinge of unease. But Darla's safety had to come first. "I'd almost rather she marry Sidney. Then I'd at least know she's safe."

"What?" Fiona exclaimed. "Don't talk like a quitter! I can't stand quitters!" She sank into a chair across from him. "One thing I won't have people saying is that I raised a bunch of lily-livered, weak-kneed men." She passed a hand over her brow, rearranging her hair a little, as if that would help reorganize her thoughts.

"There's been nothing but craziness around here for a

while. I'm sorry to say it, Aunt Fiona, but your plan has definitely not been conducive to communal calm."

Tears jumped into her eyes, brightening them as she stared at him remorsefully. "I just want the best for you and your brothers."

"I know you do," Judah said softly, "but you don't give us all the facts. You wouldn't even have told us you and Burke were married except that we figured it out."

"You boys were so young when your parents…well, you know." Fiona sniffled into a tissue for a second, then stiffened. "Burke and I made the decision that we didn't want to confuse you. He always loved you boys, but he knew he couldn't take the place of your father, nor could I take the place of your mother. We felt it was best if we always were just aunt and bodyguard to you."

"Bodyguard?" Judah frowned. "Burke isn't your bodyguard."

"He was quite the fighter in his youth," Fiona said. "A street fighter for the cause. Things changed for us when we came over here to take care of you boys. We had to make fast decisions. Maybe we didn't make them the best we could, but I stand by them." She wiped at her eyes and put her tissue away. "I'm not going to say we didn't make mistakes. But there's a lot we didn't want to burden you children with."

"We're not children anymore."

"True," Fiona conceded. "Which is why I don't want you babbling about ghosts. You just marry Darla and raise your babies, and that'll be more than your parents were able to do for you." She sighed heavily. "People don't always get the chance to do what they really want to do."

Judah felt as if a knife had been stabbed into his gut. Never had it occurred to him that his father had been unable to raise him and his brothers. It was almost like an unbroken chain of missed parenting, he realized. The shock of being shot at, and being determined to keep his little family safe, had made him think that the best thing to do would be to let Darla have a life far away from Rancho Diablo and its spiraling misfortunes.

But should one bullet keep him and Darla apart?

He thought about the cave, and the secrets he knew were there, and the silver bar that had been in the kitchen, and the ancient Native American who visited their home every year. He thought about Sam coming after their parents were gone, as Jonas had pointed out years ago, and he wondered if it wasn't family ghosts he should fear, but far-reaching skeletons that had never rested comfortably. "I don't know," he murmured. "This isn't the way I envisioned a marriage beginning."

"That should be up to Darla, I would think. But you do what you think is best. Heaven only knows I'm all out of ideas."

Fiona left the bunkhouse, hurt and unsure, and Judah felt bad for the words he'd spoken to her. But then he got thinking about Darla for the hundredth time that day, and wondered if all his brave words about breaking up with her to protect her were really based in the fact that he'd never known a father growing up—and maybe he didn't know what being a father actually meant.

NOT THIRTY MINUTES LATER, Judah's jaw dropped when Darla wafted into the bunkhouse, wearing a blue dress and looking like something out of his most fervent dreams.

"This is the simplest decision you've ever made," Darla said. "Get up and get in my truck, Lazarus. Where's your overnight bag?"

"I'm not going anywhere," he said, just to test her, and she looked at him with a patient, determined gaze.

"Yes, you are," she said sweetly. "Because if you don't,

I'm staying here, and I'm pretty certain a lady isn't welcome among bachelor men in a bunkhouse."

Darla would be. His brothers would welcome her with open arms. They liked Darla a lot, and they would feel that if she wanted to coop up here with the father of her children and the man she'd nearly married less than twenty-four hours ago, that was certainly her priority. Shoot, they'd probably roll out a red carpet and the family crystal.

But he could think of a bunch of places he'd rather Darla be than holed up with his brothers. As a crew, they were a fairly unimpressive group. They played Scrabble, and sometimes bridge. Some of them read books by foreign authors, and sometimes they watched movies in French, not to learn the language of love so much as enjoy it. They were basically nerds, and if there was one thing Judah didn't consider himself, it was a pencil-carrying nerd. "Where are we going, and for how long?" he asked, grumbling to show her he didn't appreciate being taken charge of, though secretly he thought it was sexy.

"Just get in my truck and you'll find out."

He shoved himself off the sofa. "Did Fiona put you up to taking me off her hands? She's worried about me."

"Everyone's worried about you because you've gone weird. But Fiona doesn't know I'm rescuing you from yourself."

He blinked, hesitating as he tossed some random clothes into a duffel. "I don't need rescuing. I don't need nursing, either," he said stubbornly.

"Good, because Jackie can't take care of you and three babies and her husband, and she's the only nurse in the family I know of who'd be willing to take care of you. Can you carry that duffel or should I?"

He glared. "Only one of my arms was shot, thanks." Actually, he'd hang the bag around his neck like a Saint Bernard if he'd been shot in both arms. A man could stand to look only so weak in front of his woman.

"Good. Then come on. There's no time to waste."

"Why?" Judah strode after Darla, getting in front of her to open the driver's door for her. "What's the rush?"

"Would you believe me if I said I can't wait another minute to get my hands on you, Judah Callahan?"

He smirked. "Now that's more like it," he said, and closed the door. Tossing his duffel into the truck bed, he hurried around to get in the truck. "What took you so long?"

"So long to what?" Darla backed down the drive, waving at Sam and Jonas as they loped back to the bunkhouse, looking a little worse for wear. "What have they been doing?"

"I think they rescued Judge Julie from our longhorn." Judah squinted at his brothers, noting torn and dirty pants on both of them. "I'm kind of glad I didn't make that rescue. I wonder if they left Rafe for dead."

Darla turned on the main road. "Why would they?"

"Depends on how dead he was, and if an angel was smiling on him." Judah focused his attention on Darla, not worried about his harebrained brothers. "Anyway, what took you so long to realize you couldn't keep your hands off my rock-hard body? I should make you wait for playing hard to get." He tweaked her hair. "It would serve you right."

Darla laughed. "My, you talk big, cowboy."

Judah leaned his head back and grinned, happy to let Darla drive him to her house. "But I can back up every word, sweetheart."

"This may not be the kind of visit you think it's going to be. As you pointed out, I need protection, and so protection you're going to be," Darla told him. Judah waved at Judge Julie as they went by, and at his brother Rafe, who was lying on the ground, probably looking up the judge's tight dress—if Judah knew his brother, and he was pretty sure he did—and thought life was sweet when you had a hot blonde like Darla who was gaga for your lovemaking. Of course, if she wanted to pretend it wasn't all about the loving, and that she needed a bodyguard to keep her warm, he'd be her muscled protector—just for tonight. He'd rather keep an eye on her than listen to his brothers argue over words on the Scrabble board.

And he wouldn't be lying if he bragged that he could make love with one arm tied behind his back.

TWO HOURS LATER, Darla parked Judah in a room at the StarShine Hotel in Santa Fe. He'd protested, but he ceased his halfhearted carping when he saw that she'd reserved the honeymoon suite. She detected a fairly enthusiastic gleam in Judah's dark blue eyes, and a certain curiosity at what the little woman might be up to now.

The cowboy was in for a surprise.

"Why are we here?" he asked, in a tone that suggested he already knew, and Darla smiled at him blithely.

"It was the only room big enough for the both of us," she told him, her voice ever so sweet.

He raised a brow. "I mean, why are we in Santa Fe?"

"Oh." She waved a hand. "I knew you were worried about me being at Rancho Diablo in case someone tried to kill you, and I knew you'd be worried about being at my house in case someone tried to kill you, so I thought it'd be best to bring you someplace no one would be able to try to kill you. You know. In case someone tries to kill you." She smiled at him. "And we never planned a honeymoon, so this seems as good a place as any. I always wanted to stay here," she said, slipping off her shoes and coat. She noticed she had Judah's attention, so she pointed to the bed. "Why don't you make yourself comfortable while I take a bath? Be sure to prop that arm up."

"You didn't bring your nurse's uniform by any chance, did

you?" he asked, his tone hopeful. Trust her guy to be the one with a nurse fantasy. Darla headed for the bathroom, planning to lock herself in and draw a nice, full tub.

"I'm sorry. I'm off duty. But you don't need anyone to take care of you," she called. "You just relax and let me know if anyone comes to the door."

"Are we expecting someone?" Judah asked.

"No. But just in case someone does come and tries to, you know, shoot you or something. I don't want to be in the tub when it happens."

She thought she heard him mutter, and smiled to herself.

Thirty minutes later, when she came out of the bathroom, Judah was sound asleep, which had been her plan all along. She grabbed her robe and her things and slipped into the room across the hall, locking the door behind her.

JUDAH AWAKENED twelve hours later, if his watch was right. He thumped on it to make certain it was still working. Apparently it was, because it corresponded to the clock radio next to the bed, which Darla had tossed a towel over for reasons he couldn't decipher.

Had he made love to her? Was that why he'd slept so long? Nope, he hadn't had so much as a kiss or anything pleasant like that. He passed a hand over his stubble, testing his arm. It was sore as hell, but not so sore that he couldn't pleasure Darla to the depths of her being.

So what had gone wrong with his little lady's seduction?

He felt the bed beside him, patting around for a soft, round body. There was time enough before checkout to give Darla a rousing dose of what she'd clearly wanted last night. After all, he was a stud, not a dud.

There was no sexy, warm female next to him, and the bed felt suspiciously undisturbed on her side. He flipped on the bedside lamp, realizing that not only had he not made love to Darla, she hadn't even slept in the room.

He tapped his watch again. No, twelve hours really had elapsed, and she hadn't spent them with him.

Which made him wonder if he'd said something to upset her. "Bath," he said, "and I fell asleep. Possibly I should have offered to bathe with her, but she seemed determined to be alone."

So that wasn't the problem.

"I'm pretty sure I shouldn't have been sleeping alone," he muttered, and went to find Darla. There was a door that looked as if it connected to another room in the suite, so he banged on that, and a moment later she opened it, wearing a stunner of a white nightie. His breath left him.

"Yes?" Darla said, and he frowned.

"Why are you in there?"

"Where else would I be?"

He took in her pretty pink toenails, and sweet lace in a V down her front, almost to her belly. In fact, if she shifted just right, perhaps he could see a little bit more of Darla. The peekaboo effect really had his attention, so he decided to play it soft and smooth. "Shouldn't you be with me? In that nice comfy bed?"

She shook her head. "No, that's a honeymoon suite. I'm not on my honeymoon."

"Oh," he said, "*that's* what this is about. You're annoyed." He had a sneaking suspicion he was caught in a plot, which shouldn't be happening in a honeymoon suite.

Other things should be happening, like lovemaking.

"Any chance I can convince you to let me order you breakfast in bed?"

She smiled. "I'd like that. Ask them to bring it to the B suite."

He glanced over his shoulder. "Am I in the A side?"

"Yes," she said, her tone like cotton candy. "A is for ass."

He blinked. "Oh. This isn't a weekend for seduction. This is about showing me what I'm missing out on."

"I always knew you were smart, cowboy." Darla smiled at him, and his gut tightened. "We could be on a honeymoon, but we're not, because of a tiny bit of lead. We could be making love, but we're not, because you broke up with me, because of a fractional piece of lead. And so," she said, "I'm sleeping without a husband, which I hate, because I really had my sights set on a certain cowboy. And so my children will be born without their father's last name, all because of a teeny weeny, miniscule—"

"That's it," Judah said. "If you went to the trouble of getting a honeymoon suite, you probably also went to the trouble of making certain there was a justice of the peace around who would marry us after you drove me insane with that bridal nightie."

Darla smiled. "Maybe."

"Did you bring a dress and all the rigmarole a bride needs? I'd hate for you to marry me without feeling like a real bride." Ten years from now, would she look back on their marriage as a quickie, low-budget affair? He tried to buck himself up to hero status in her eyes. "If you're determined to do this, we could fly to Hawaii."

She handed him a menu. "Order breakfast. You'll need it to fortify yourself for giving up your bachelorhood. Fiona packed your tux. You'll find it hanging in the cabinet. I can't wait for Hawaii, Judah, because you might get shot. Although I can get you a bulletproof vest for under your tux, if you're worried."

She closed the door.

"I'd like to think she's worried about me being shot," Judah muttered, "but I think she's trying to tell me something."

He went to order breakfast and then locate the tux the

little woman had thoughtfully commandeered on his behalf. Who was he to tell a lady wearing a white lacy nightie that he wouldn't run through a hail of bullets for just one night in her bed?

Chapter Sixteen

Fiona peeped in after Darla closed the connecting door between suite A and suite B. Jackie followed, as did Aberdeen, and Darla's mother, Mavis, with Corinne and Nadine waiting behind them. All her friends were here, and for Darla, sandbagging Judah like this couldn't have been more perfect.

"Is he gone?" Fiona asked.

"With his marching orders," Darla said. "Come in."

"We'll get you into this beautiful gown post haste," Jackie said, "though I'm not afraid Judah's going to change his mind."

Darla wasn't afraid of that, either. Not anymore. If she'd learned anything, it was that her man was stubborn and opinionated, and if Fiona said he really wanted to be caught, because he was too worried about the danger to Darla to go willingly, then maybe she was on to something.

"Judah did say once that he'd never be caught dead at an altar," Darla said as Jackie eased her into the magic wedding dress, and Fiona said, "Well, he nearly was dead at the altar, so he was almost right, for once. We're just not going to tempt Fate a second time."

"If it wasn't for the children," Darla said, "getting married wouldn't matter to me so much." But the instant she said the words, she knew it wasn't true. The magic wedding gown sparkled on her, drew in light, making her catch her breath. "I love him," she murmured. "I always have."

"I know," Jackie said. "That's why this time we're not taking any chances. It's all about the gown."

It was true. The moment she'd waited for was here, and right. Deep inside herself, she knew Judah wasn't afraid of marrying her, he was afraid of hurting her. "Thank you all so much for helping me," Darla said. "I treasure your friendship more than you can ever know." She hugged her mother, and then, hearing Judah pound on the door adjoining their rooms, said, "You hide in here until we've left."

The ladies concealed themselves in the large bathroom and the huge walk-in closet, and Darla opened the door. Judah, just as handsome as he'd been last night in his tux, stared at her. "New gown?"

"The one from last time had a few bloodstains on it," Darla said. "I thought I'd wear something else for good luck."

"The luck is all mine. Wow." His eyes glittered as he took her in. "We could see how fast I can get you out of that gown now, and then go to the J.P."

"No, thank you," Darla said quickly, more than aware of the listening ears concealed in her room. "I'm not sure what time the office closes."

Judah nodded. "That's probably a wise plan, but you know, you could change my mind. I'm easy."

"I know." Darla was blushing all over, and if she ever got the nerve to tell Judah where the wedding guests had been hiding, he would probably blush, too.

Or maybe he'd just be proud of himself.

"Then I guess we're going to run this route," Judah said, "if you're sure you want to marry me."

"I'm not one hundred percent certain," Darla said coyly, "particularly as you once told me that marriage was for whipped men, and you wouldn't be caught dead doing it."

"Got you into bed that night, didn't I, though?" Judah kissed her hand as Darla blushed again. "I knew you were the kind of girl who just couldn't resist a challenge."

"Come on," she said, knowing that later on she was going to get a lot of teasing from her lady friends—and heaven only knew what her mother thought about everything she was hearing. Fiona was probably shocked, too.

Judah smiled at her. "You're the most beautiful bride I've ever seen."

"Really?" Darla asked. "Have you seen many?"

"My fair share," her sexy rascal of a man said, "but somehow, you're the only woman who's ever made me feel like getting married is magical."

"Let's go before the magic wears off, then," Darla said, and Judah just smiled as he took her hand. He walked past the closet and banged on it, and then the bathroom door and banged on that, too, and said, "Ladies, don't be late to the wedding!" and Darla wondered if he'd just played hard to get to see if she wanted him enough to drag him to the altar.

He was the most infuriating man she'd ever known—and she was head over heels in love with him.

JUDAH WASN'T CERTAIN why he knew this moment was the best of his life, but the second that Darla Cameron said "I do" he felt like a new man. A better man. He couldn't have explained the emotions that swept over him as he watched her face while she spoke the words. All he knew was that something he'd waited for all his life had just agreed to be a part of him forever, and it was a very precious thing. He couldn't imagine not having Darla beside him at this moment and every other, and when he slipped the ring on her finger and she gazed up at him with wide, beautiful eyes, he just knew the moment was magic.

And he wanted it to last forever.

WEEKS AFTER THE WEDDING, gifts were still arriving at Darla's house, which now contained one cowboy husband and a bunch of well-wishers. Of course, everyone in Diablo wanted to know why she and Judah had married out of town. Darla simply told everyone that they'd decided to take a leaf from Aberdeen and Creed's wedding manual. Folks were satisfied with that, except that they were dying to see a wedding at Rancho Diablo.

Her house had become a shrine to weddings and babies. Darla had never seen so many presents. "These children will lack for nothing," she told Judah, and he grinned as he unwrapped a pair of tiny pink snakeskin cowboy boots.

Then the smile slipped from his face. "Wait. Why are these pink, Darla?"

She glanced over at the boots. "I don't know, but they're darling."

"I know that." He studied them, mystified. "But they should be blue. Blue is for boys. My sons will not be wearing pink boots, even if they're in a cradle where I can cover them with a blanket."

Darla laughed. "Babies don't wear cowboy boots in a cradle. They're for later on. Toddler age."

"We'll have to take these back."

Darla put down the crystal bowl she'd just unwrapped and went to look at the card. "The boots are from your brothers. Every single one of them signed the card. And there are two pairs of boots." She giggled. "I never realized the Callahans are so into gag gifts."

"I'm tired of gag gifts," Judah grumbled.

Darla looked at him. "What do you mean?" she said, wondering if he was referring to the gag gift that had brought them together in the first place.

Judah dropped the boots back into the box. "Uh-uh," he said, "you're not going to catch me that easily. I love gag gifts.

I love my brothers' insane sense of humor." He kissed her cheek, her neck, finding his way to the buttons of her dress, which he casually popped open. "Don't worry that I meant the original, granddaddy of them all gag gift, because I didn't."

"You'd better not." She pulled away from his interested perusal of her cleavage. "Keep unboxing. We have a lot of thank-you letters to write."

"This house isn't going to be big enough for all of us and all this stuff," Judah pointed out.

Darla smiled. "Jackie and Aberdeen warned me this conversation would come up."

"Why?" He shook his head. "By the way, I'm not writing the thank-you letter for these pink boots. You can do that one."

Darla ignored his anxiety over the baby-girl boots. "Because somehow Jackie and Aberdeen said they found themselves eventually moving out to Rancho Diablo. I intend to hold firm, however."

"But it's such a great place to live." Judah held up a fluffy white baby blanket embroidered with a pink giraffe. "Why are we receiving pink things, Darla? Am I the last one in town to know something?"

She giggled. "It would be both of us. Unless my doctor has dropped a hint…"

They stared at each other.

"He wouldn't have," Darla said.

Judah shook his head. "No. Doc Graybill wouldn't."

"Unless Fiona wormed it out of him," Darla said.

Judah started to deny the possibility, then closed his mouth.

Darla sighed. "Let me know if anybody gives us something blue. But you see, there are reasons not to live at Rancho Diablo while we're still getting to know each other, Judah."

He gave her a look of innocence. "Did I ever hint that I wanted to move to the ranch?"

"You just claimed my house is too small."

"It is," Judah said, "but I like being as close to you as possible, Mrs. Callahan. In fact, I'd like to be a lot closer. Let's downsize and get a smaller house and a much smaller bed." He grabbed her around the waist, lifting her so that she had to put down the gift she'd been unwrapping, after which he carried her to the bedroom.

Darla laughed, enjoying her husband's antics, thinking that there was nothing more wonderful than making love with Judah on a summer afternoon in August. But then pain sliced across her belly, and she doubled up. Worried, Darla waited for the pain to go away.

"What happened? Are you all right?" Judah asked, leaning over her as she took deep breaths through her nose, trying to stay calm.

Another cramp racked her. "Probably just a little baby kick or two. Maybe we're having dancers. I don't think it's something I ate."

"We had oatmeal," he said. "Plain organic oatmeal with a tiny bit of brown sugar, nothing exciting, so that means, Darla, my love, that you get a trip in my chariot to see the doctor. We'll let him tell us if you've got garden variety gas cramps. Or just a lot of baby fun going on in there."

"I think you're right," Darla said, letting Judah lead her past the presents to the door, feeling her whole world shake around her.

"I'M NO COWARD," Judah told his brothers, who'd gathered around him to wait at the hospital, where Darla had been instantly sent by her concerned doctor, "but I'm shaking like a leaf right now. And if somebody doesn't come out of that room soon and tell me something about my wife, I'm going Rambo."

"Easy," Jonas said. "Darla needs you in a Zen state, not all whacked out. Everything's going to be fine."

"You're a cardiac guy, what the hell do you know about that end of the female body, anyway?" Judah snapped, appreciating his brother trying to ease his fears, but unable to do anything but bite down on any hand that reached out to comfort him. Like a feral wolf. That's how he felt: feral, primitive, caged. This is when he ran. Always separating himself from fear, anxiety, doubt.

This time he couldn't. He had to sit here and wait. Darla wasn't far enough along to be having the babies. He knew that, though Jonas hadn't proffered any professional opinion. Judah had seen his brother hanging around the nurses' station, ferreting information out of them. Medical terminology was way over Judah's head at the moment. He wanted a simple "your wife is fine, your babies are fine."

He wanted to be with Darla, but Darla had said she wanted him to stay in the waiting room. Had insisted.

The anxiety was killing him. He wondered why she hadn't wanted him with her. Shouldn't a wife want her husband? If he didn't hear something soon, he was going to make everybody mad by barging into his wife's room, and damn the consequences. Of all people, Darla knew best that he wasn't a patient worrier. He wasn't patient about anything.

At least he had his brothers with him to wait this agony out. "So, you guys are butts for giving Darla and me pink cowboy boots."

"You're having two babies," Sam pointed out. "We thought it was a priceless idea. Rafe came up with that one. I was rooting for pink baby dolls, but then Rafe suggested pink ropers and we immediately ordered them."

Judah grunted. "Why not blue?"

His brothers smirked at him.

"Why would you be the one to have the boys in this family?" Creed asked.

"A precedent has been set, if you haven't noticed," Pete

said, "and we figure gambler's odds on pink being the order of the day."

"We'll see about that." He'd be happy to have babies of either sex—babies born healthy and yelling the ears off the nurses, though not tonight. They weren't quite ready to come out of the maternal oven. "What could be taking so long? Darla was just having a bit of a stomach ache."

The brothers turned their gazes to Jonas, who shrugged.

He was saved from answering by the doctor coming out. "Mr. Callahan?" he said, and all the brothers said, "Yes?"

"Sorry," Rafe said, "we're strung tighter than guitars. This is Dad." He pointed to Judah, who stood, with nervous pangs attacking him.

"I'm Darla's husband," he said. "These are my brothers."

"Why don't you step back here so we can talk, Mr. Callahan?" the doctor suggested. "I'm Dr. Feske."

"Can I see my wife?" Judah asked.

"You can, but let's talk first." They settled in a small room, and from the unsmiling expression on Dr. Feske's face, Judah knew the news wasn't good.

"Is Darla all right?"

"Your wife is fine. Your daughters were born prematurely—"

Judah tried to bat back the small specks of blackness dancing in front of his eyes. "Prematurely? They've hardly had time to grow."

"The success rate with preemies is quite good, though they'll be in the hospital for some time."

"Is something wrong?" Judah pressed his palms together, trying to keep his hands from shaking.

"We're running tests to make certain everything is as it should be, in the range for the amount of time they spent—"

"Doctor," Judah interrupted, "is Darla all right?"

He nodded. "Mr. Callahan, the prognosis is good for your

entire family. Yes, the babies are young, but they seem well-developed and within the norm for what—"

"I'm sorry," Judah said. "But I can only take in about half of what you're saying, and I really need to see my wife." He wasn't certain he'd ever felt this desperate in his life. Fear gnawed at him, driving him crazy.

"I understand, Mr. Callahan. Would you like to see your wife, or visit the neonatal—"

"Darla," Judah said. "I need to see my wife."

The doctor led him to Darla's room. She was pale, and had a sheet pulled up to her neck.

"Hey, beautiful," Judah said. "How do you feel?"

"Like I've been through a washer." She looked at him as he tucked a strand of her hair behind her ear. "Have you seen the babies? What do you think?"

"I came to see you first." Judah kissed her forehead, then her lips.

"Well, apparently your daughters were anxious to see you," Darla told him. "They get their impatience from the Callahan side of the tree."

He tried to smile for her sake. "Everything's going to be fine."

"I know," Darla said. "They're Callahans. They're tough."

Judah nodded, his throat tight. He hoped so. God, how he hoped so.

Chapter Seventeen

When Judah saw his daughters ten minutes later, he honestly thought his heart stopped. He felt for his chest, wondering if he'd imagined a skipped beat. His daughters weren't tough at all. They were tiny, half the size of footballs maybe, with more tubes than a baby should endure taped to teeny appendages.

He wanted to cry. Pete's daughters had gone longer in the womb than these, and at their birth, Judah had been totally unnerved by those tiny little babies. He was overcome now by the urge to hold his daughters, but he knew he couldn't.

He had to stay strong for Darla.

"You're as beautiful as your mother," he told his twin girls through the glass. "You don't know this now, but she's a nurse. She can help you grow big and strong."

Then his shoulders began to shake, and he started to cry, wondering what he could have done differently to help his tiny babies grow. The doctor didn't have to lie to him. Judah could tell that these babies might not make it, and if they did, they might not be strong, barrel-racing, boot-scooting cowgirls. "You've got me on your team," he told them, "and I'm a big, tough guy. Daddy won't let anything happen to you. Nothing at all."

But he thought they needed guardian angels, too.

"Don't worry," a voice said next to him.

Judah turned, startled to see Fiona's Native American friend standing at his side.

"Do not worry," he said, his black eyes sure and calm as he met Judah's gaze. "These are blessings, and they are meant to be here. They are meant to make you strong."

Judah blinked. "You mean, I must make them strong."

"No." He went back to perusing the tiny bassinets.

After a moment, he surprised Judah by taking out an iPhone and snapping a picture. "I will say prayers," he told Judah, and then ambled down the hall.

Judah stared after the man, who disappeared around the corner before he had a chance to say anything else, stunned as he was by the sudden visit. Then he glanced back at his daughters, his gaze searching, but strangely enough, he felt calmer now.

"I'm going to go take care of your mother," Judah told his daughters. "But I'll be back. Every day you'll see my face at this window. For now you just rest, and when you're ready, I'll be here to hold you. Daddy will always be around to hold you, until finally it's your turn to take care of me."

Judah loped off to find his wife. It was just beginning to hit him that he was a father now, for real. Those tiny bundles were his, and he felt as if he'd just been handed the world's biggest trophy and the shiniest buckle ever made.

"HE'S CHANGED," Fiona told Burke a week later. "I don't know what's come over Judah, but he's seems in permanent 'ohm' mode. Have you noticed the calmer, more relaxed Judah? When he's not at the hospital, that is."

"Guess he likes being a father." Burke put away the last of the dishes and smiled at her. "He just didn't know how much he would, maybe."

"He's different." Fiona considered her nephew with some pleasure. "Nothing rattles him anymore. He never even mentions being shot. I've got the ballistics report from the sheriff, but Judah never talks about what happened that night, so I'm sure not going to bring it up."

Burke shrugged. "The shooting wasn't important to Judah, as long as Darla was fine. I think he believes it was an accident, and if it wasn't, Sheriff Cartwright'll let him know. All Judah cares about is that he married Darla with no static from next door, and he has his daughters. That's all that matters to him." Burke looked over Fiona's shoulder at the paper she held. "So what does it say?"

"That the gun was a .38. It's not registered to Bode or anybody else in this town. Likely it was black market." Fiona frowned, her thoughts moving from the pleasant aspect of her two new great-nieces to the rumblings on the ranch. "Which scares me, because it means we don't know what we're dealing with. It's a new element. I was hoping it was Bode," she said, "because we could have easily handled him."

Burke frowned. "Does the sheriff have any theories?"

"They found no footprints, and no new vehicles coming through town that they noticed that night or since. No one's been in town asking questions, and nobody has contacted the sheriff's office with any tips. And everyone knows about the shooting, because most of Diablo was there. So if somebody strange was hanging around, Sheriff Cartwright would get a call in a hurry."

"Why would someone we don't know want to take a potshot at Judah?" Burke asked.

Fiona and he looked at each other for a long time.

Then they turned back to cleaning the kitchen, both to their own tasks, without saying another word.

SINCE DARLA HAD REQUIRED a C-section, her mother and all her friends wanted to come over and take care of her. Judah found he didn't have as much time alone with his wife as he wished, thanks to the steady stream of callers. He'd asked Darla if she'd like for him to start screening her visitors a bit, trim her social time, so she could rest—and so he could spend some time with her.

Darla had said she enjoyed the company and knew he needed to be working, so he might as well go do what he had to do and let everybody else look in on her if they wanted to. He'd tried to act as if he had a whole lot he could be doing, but the truth was, his brothers were covering for him, and shooed him away from the chores if he ever came to help.

It was getting depressing. There was nothing for him to do at the hospital except stare through the glass at his daughters, and because he was there so much, it seemed to him that they never grew. He didn't detect any changes at all, which gave him the nearest thing to a panic attack he could ever recall having.

In fact, staring at his babies and not being able to do anything to help them was worse than a bad ride. He'd rather be thrown any day of the week than be helpless, as he was now.

And Darla didn't want him hanging around. That much was clear. She said she had "lady" moments he couldn't help with, which he'd decided was code for *I'm trying to figure out pumping breast milk, so I need Jackie and Aberdeen more than you right now.*

Although he would have been more than happy to help with that. He was pretty sure Darla's breasts were a lot bigger right now, and he wouldn't have minded reacquainting himself with them, which he supposed was a chauvinistic thought, except that he missed his wife and wanted to feel he had some connection with her.

He felt like a roommate. He wasn't even sleeping with her, having banished himself to a guest room so she could rest, and so he wouldn't accidentally turn over in the night, forget and reach for her, and crush her stitches or something.

He didn't know if she had stitches. He wasn't certain how a C-section was performed, exactly. He did feel that his wife was in a fragile state right now, and the best thing he could do was not roll over on her in his sleep.

But she hadn't invited him into her room, either.

Forced away from chores on the ranch and outnumbered by females in his house, Judah slunk off to the bunkhouse to try to center himself. He flung himself onto the leather sofa and closed his eyes in complete appreciation of the quietude.

Which lasted all of five minutes before the door blew open on a strong gust of wind. Judah didn't open his eyes until he realized the door hadn't closed.

He sighed upon seeing his visitor. "It would be you, Tunstall. An ill wind blows no good."

"Your brothers said I'd find you here," Sidney said. "Mind if I talk to you?"

Judah sat up and motioned to the sofa. "Sit."

He waited for Sidney to unload. Hopefully, this was about anything other than Darla. Right now, Judah wasn't in the mood to discuss his wife, or his life, or much of anything. He didn't even want company.

"Congratulations on the twins," Sidney said.

"No doubt you wish Darla was married to you. Probably, you figure that as a doctor, you could care for them better than I can," Judah said sourly.

"Problems?" Sidney asked.

"Do I look like I'm having problems?"

"You always look like you're having problems, Judah." Sidney smiled. "Your daughters are going to be fine."

Judah crooked a brow. "Do you think so? Or are you just blowing smoke up my ass for your own nefarious purposes?"

"Now, Callahan," Sidney said. "Darla told me you were having a few little worries about your girls. I just came to reassure you."

Judah grimaced. "Because you're a pediatrician or a wizard, and know so much."

Sidney shook his head. "Look. I know all this animosity isn't because of Darla. I know you're worried. Darla loves you. She just wants you to lighten up so she can quit worrying about *you.*"

"Did she send you to tell me this or are you applying for a job as a marriage counselor?" Judah couldn't have said why he was so ornery. Pretty much anything Tunstall said was going to rile him. His brothers could give testimony to the fact that just about everything annoyed Judah lately. "Okay," he finally said. "I'll admit I'm a little worked up. But that doesn't mean I want you here ladling out advice and words of comfort I don't need."

Sidney nodded. "All right."

"So you can go." Judah waved a hand toward the door.

"I haven't finished."

Judah raised a brow. "Then would you get on with it? I don't have all day to listen to your clichés."

Sidney laughed. "You really have it bad, don't you?"

"Have what bad?" He frowned.

"Never mind," the doctor said. "Listen, what I wanted to ask you is…" He lowered his voice, even though there was no one else in the bunkhouse. "Well, I've been talking to Diane lately. And I was wondering—"

Judah held up a hand. "No. You can't marry her to fulfill the terms of that inheritance that's hanging over your head. Diane isn't Darla. Darla was being…well, she was trying to be helpful because she's like that, and you caught her at a difficult time in her life, and…I don't want to talk about it."

"I wasn't talking about Darla. You were," Sidney said. "All I want to know is if you think Diane is ready to date. I didn't say I wanted to marry her. Jeez."

Judah lowered his eyelids, considering him through slitted eyes. "You're kind of a snake in the grass, aren't you?"

"I resent that!"

Sidney really did sound riled. Judah grunted, realizing he'd drawn blood, when he hadn't drawn any with all the other barbs he'd flung at the doc. "All right. Why Diane?"

"I like her," Sidney said with a sudden flush of his angled cheekbones. "I like her little girls."

"Those are Creed and Aberdeen's little girls, too," Judah said. "And Diane is… I don't know about Diane. Why the hell are you asking me?"

Sidney shrugged. "I'd like to do this right." He stood. "Anyway, sorry to take up your time. Good luck with the twins and—"

"Hang on a minute," Judah said, motioning for him to sit back down. "Don't go off all offended."

"I'm not offended," Sidney said. "You're always a little rude, but I understand why."

"I am not rude," Judah stated. "I pride myself on being a gentleman."

"Whatever," Sidney said. "As long as Darla sees that side of you, I don't care how you are."

Judah took a long, hard look at his one-time rival. "Diane had a difficult road to hoe. If you ask her out, you take good care of her. Which I know you will," he said generously. "You're an okay guy, and I'd probably feel all right about you if you hadn't tried to marry my girl."

"Darla wasn't your girl," Sidney said, "and as I recall, at that time you had your head so far up your ass you couldn't see daylight. Darla didn't want to be unmarried and pregnant. This is a very small town, and everyone knows her and her mother, and that's why she was willing to help me out. But it had nothing to do with love or sex or anything but a bargain between friends. You were not her friend, you were a butthead, and she wasn't going to sit around and wait for you."

Judah listened to Sidney's soliloquy, then shook his head. "I've been in love with that woman for years."

Sidney's eyebrows shot up. "Are you serious?"

Judah nodded. "Yep."

"Does…Darla know this?"

"I don't think so," Judah said, trying to remember if he'd ever gotten around to telling her that she'd held his heart for so long he'd sometimes thought he might not ever get it back. "Things have been moving pretty fast."

"Yeah, well." Sidney walked to the door. "If I had a prescription to offer you, it would be to sit down and talk to your wife instead of hiding out over here. You don't want to be in the bunkhouse, you want to be with Darla."

Judah nodded. It was true, and the fact that he didn't want to stomp Sidney's head in for implying he wasn't handling his love life very well was a great sign. "Hey, good luck with Diane."

Sidney smiled. "Thanks." He disappeared out the door.

Judah got to his feet, took a deep breath and turned off the lamps.

It was time to go home. It was past time for some honesty between him and the lovely Mrs. Judah Callahan.

If he could shoo all the well-meaning friends and family out of the henhouse.

Chapter Eighteen

When Judah entered the house, Darla was surrounded by about sixteen ladies giving her a baby shower. He walked in tall, dark and handsome—and Darla could tell at once that something was wrong with her man.

He looked darker than usual.

"Hi, Judah," Darla said.

"Have some punch, Judah," Fiona added, handing him a crystal cup filled with pink liquid.

"And a cucumber sandwich." Mavis passed him a plate with tiny, triangle-shaped, crustless sandwiches. Judah looked perturbed, as if he didn't know what to do with such insubstantial food.

"And a petit four," Corinne Abernathy said. "The frosting is so sweet it'll give you a cavity on contact. But it's so good!" She put two on a tiny dish she stacked on the other plate he was holding.

Nadine Waters handed him a pink napkin. "We decided to decorate the nursery. Which meant a shopping spree! And of course, a small party."

Darla smiled at Judah. He looked overwhelmed, ready to flee. And she didn't want him to go anywhere. She wanted him to stay and relax for a change. He never relaxed around her; he never relaxed *here.* She was pretty certain he had complete fish-out-of-water syndrome in her house.

"Let me show you what the ladies did for our nursery, Judah." She got up, and Judah practically dropped all his plates, plus the crystal cup, rushing to press her back down on the sofa.

"Don't get up. You're supposed to be resting," he said. "In fact, I'm not sure all this excitement is good for you."

"I'm fine," Darla said with some exasperation. "I'm not made of china."

"I can find the nursery myself," he said, tipping his hat at the ladies as he escaped down the hall. He'd left his food untouched on the table, and Darla suspected he was happy to be away from all the females.

"Excuse me," she said to her friends. "I have to go tend to my husband. I hate to cut this short—it's been lovely—but I need to settle him down or he'll never feel like this is home."

Fiona grinned. "We completely understand. We'll clean up in here, and you go calm a cowboy."

"Thank you." She looked around at her friends. "I can never thank you enough for everything you've done. And the nursery is a dream come true."

Corinne touched her hand. "We'll be quiet as mice, so don't mind us at all."

Darla went down the hall. Judah wasn't in the nursery; the door hadn't been opened. She found him in the guest room, sitting on the bed he'd commandeered for his own. "Hey, husband," she said.

"Hi." He glanced up morosely. "You should be resting. Not having company all the time."

She sat down next to him. "Judah, I can take care of myself."

"I'd like to take care of you."

She gingerly put her face against his. "You need to work. The ladies are happy to keep me from losing my mind while my babies can't be here."

"I can be here." Judah allowed her to stroke his cheek, then caught her fingertips and pressed them to his lips, kissing them. "I want to be here."

"And I want your life to go on as it was, unchanged, until our daughters come home. I want you to stop worrying. There's nothing you can do here, Judah. I'm learning about my body, and healing, and figuring out why some parts of me work differently than they used to. Some of it's a little strange. I'm a bit embarrassed by it all."

"Why?" He lay down, pulling her alongside him and cradling her head on his shoulder. "I want to get to know my wife."

"All right. No more company. You can do everything for me from now on. You can help me pump breast milk—"

"You're not scaring me."

Darla smiled. "And you can watch me while I nap, which is a lot of excitement—"

"I can do that."

"And you can help write our thank-you letters for all the wedding and baby shower gifts."

He leaned down to kiss her. "We don't have to go all crazy."

Laughing, she pushed him away so she could recline on his shoulder again. "You don't want to be stuck here all the time. You'd be bored out of your skull. You're a man of action, not a couch cowboy."

"True," he said, "but if I can talk you into being naked, and just the two of us watching soaps together, I could learn to like being king of the couch."

"Ugh." She closed her eyes. "I'm not going to be the queen of the couch. I can't wait to get back in my jeans so I can ride my horse."

"Let's move out to the ranch," Judah said. "There's a bunkhouse that we're not using for anything right now. We could call it home. Then I wouldn't be away from my job. You'd be there and I'd be there, and we'd have more room, and the babies would have all the family and friends around they could stand."

"I thought the ranch might be sold."

"Maybe," Judah said, "but I've got faith in Sam. He's got a lot of aces in his boot. But even if it was, we'd still be together."

"Just homeless," Darla said, loving the fact that she and Judah were lying together, dreaming about the future, comfortable with one another. This was how she wanted it to be. She wanted them to slowly grow together and bond.

"Do you doubt me, wife?" Judah cuddled her, kissing her neck—but not touching her.

"I won't break if you hold me, Judah."

"You can't lure me that easily. The doctor said rest, and rest you shall do." He nipped her neck lightly, then moved back to her lips. "Quit avoiding the subject."

Darla gave a small moan, wishing she were healed and that she could make love to her husband. "What subject was that?" she asked, distracted with lust from all Judah's kisses. *I could fly, he makes me feel so light, so gauzy.*

So in love.

"Do you doubt my ability to provide for you?"

"No," she said. "When were we talking about that? I never asked you to provide for me."

He sighed. "Typical new-age female."

She kissed his forehead, troubled but not sure why. "Typical old-fashioned male."

"Darn right," he said, and then Darla drifted off to sleep, vaguely aware that she'd missed something important, but not sure what.

WHEN DARLA AWAKENED, Judah had slipped away. The sun was shining brightly outside, and birds were singing, and—

"Heck," she said, and hopped from the bed. She remembered what they'd been talking about. He wanted to move to the ranch. She'd been giddy with lust.

"Yes, Virginia, females lust. At least I do, for Judah," she muttered, and jumped in the shower. She bathed carefully around the stitches, glad that Judah wouldn't ever see her like this—she wasn't about to let him—and then put on a comfy, oversize pair of shorts and a T-shirt that she would normally only wear for cleaning.

She went into the nursery, doubtful that Judah had even glanced in here to see the ladies' handiwork. He wasn't coping well with the fact that his daughters had come early. None of it was real yet—or he was scared. Men like Judah avoided what bothered them.

But it was a beautiful nursery now, all pink iced confections gracing smooth white furniture. She couldn't wait to bring her daughters home. Their new room was like a music box, and—

Judah hadn't looked at this room because it wasn't real. In fact, this wasn't his home. He wasn't comfortable here, and he never would be.

She was going to have to fix the situation, if they were ever going to truly be two halves of a whole.

FIONA WRINKLED HER NOSE and hung up the phone. "Judah Callahan, what have you done to that wife of yours?"

He blinked, caught in the act of lifting a piece of pound cake from the covered glass pedestal as he headed out to the barn. "Let me think about it." Squinting, he took a bite of fragrant cake, sighing with happiness. "Haven't done anything to my wife. Doctor's orders."

"That's not what I meant," Fiona said. "Corinne just called and said Darla is listing her house with her."

"Listing her house?"

"As in preparing to sell it." His aunt put her hands on her hips. "When we left that house last night, you two were supposed to be cozy as bugs in a rug."

"We were." Judah raised his cake to her. "This is delicious."

"Then why is she selling her house?"

"Beats me." He shrugged. "I've never understood the mysteries of the female mind. And that includes yours, Aunt." He kissed her cheek. "Though I do love you."

She brushed him back. "If she moves farther away from me, I'll be annoyed with you. You go over there right now and be a gentleman. Tell her you don't want her to move."

"I can't," Judah said. "She has a mind of her own."

"Did you tell her you wanted her to move?" Fiona shot him a suspicious glance.

"Yes, but..." He stopped, put down the cake. "But she wouldn't do that for me." Would she? "I asked Darla to move to the ranch, and she'd said she didn't want to in case we lost the place, and then I asked her if she doubted my ability to provide. And that was that," he said. "Honest. Moving barely came up."

Fiona glared. "You can't guilt your wife into moving when she doesn't even have her babies home from the hospital, Judah. She hasn't recovered from giving birth!"

He felt like a heel. "I admit it probably wasn't the right time to bring up the topic."

"And now she's listed her house." Fiona shook her head. "You need to tell Darla that she doesn't have to sell it."

"Why?" Judah asked. "Isn't it a good thing that she's willing to make me happy?"

Fiona closed her eyes for a second. When she opened them again, she just shrugged. "Nephew, you'll have to figure this one out on your own."

Which didn't sound good, if Fiona wasn't in the mood to dish out wise counsel. It sounded as if she was adopting a new, mind-my-own-business strategy, and Judah knew that could only mean one thing.

He had stepped in it big time.

"Hey," Jonas said as he walked by.

"Hey." Judah fell in beside his brother. "If you might possibly be in the doghouse with your lady, but you're not sure, and yet you don't want to be in the doghouse if you're not actually there—"

"Jeez," Jonas said, "I haven't had my coffee yet. Could you speak in some other format besides riddle?"

"I'm not sure if Darla is making a big decision because of me," Judah said, following his brother into the barn. "I don't want her doing something she'll regret. So I'm wondering how to approach this. Is it a flowers situation? Or a turquoise bracelet situation?"

"Boy, you're dumb," Jonas said. "The fact that you're even asking shows that you have no idea of the workings of the female mind. What did you do to Darla?"

"I didn't do anything to her!" Judah was up-to-here with everyone assuming that he'd done something to his wife. "All I said was that we should move out to the ranch. Next thing I know, she's put a call in to list her house. I hear all this from Fiona. Darla didn't tell me."

Jonas slumped on a hay bale. "The problem is that you're slow."

Judah hesitated. "Slow?"

"Slow to figure things out." He waved a hand majestically. "Obviously Darla thinks you're an ape and is moving as far away from you as possible."

Judah's heart nearly stopped. "I did not do anything to upset my wife!"

"Did you ask her?"

He shook his head. "No."

"If you did, she'd probably tell you that she liked her little house, but since you used faulty condoms and got her pregnant, now she's going to have to sell her house and live out of a cardboard box with you."

"Cardboard box?" Judah blinked. "Rancho Diablo is no cardboard box."

"Yeah, well, that's if it doesn't become Rancho Bode." Jonas shrugged. "I guess she's taking a leap of faith that you'll provide."

That's what he'd asked her: if she doubted his ability to provide for her. Judah felt a little guilty about that.

"So, I'm guessing turquoise bracelet, huh?" Judah asked, and Jonas sighed.

"I'd go ahead and make it sapphires," his brother said. "And make good friends with the jeweler. I have a feeling your marriage is going to require a frequent-shopper discount."

Judah snorted. "Why am I asking you? You've never even had a girlfriend," he said, and stomped off.

Jonas was wrong.

But just in case, maybe it wouldn't hurt to make a quick stop on the way to Darla's.

WHEN JUDAH GOT TO Darla's house, the place was empty. No note, no nothing. A shiver ran across his scalp. He didn't even have her cell phone number.

Jackie did. He could ask her, but then everyone would know that he and Darla hadn't gotten to the point of even exchanging information, and he'd look pretty much a dope, which was how he felt at the moment.

He didn't know if she was at the bridal shop or the hospital. "She's not supposed to be out of the house," he muttered. "Doctor's orders."

Fear jumped into him, and he hurried to his truck. What if she'd had a problem? What if something had gone wrong and he hadn't been here to help her? After he'd sent her friends and family away, and made a big deal of how he could take care of her, he hadn't even bothered to ask for her cell number.

He tore down the driveway and nearly collided with Jackie's truck as she was pulling in. Darla was in the front seat. He was relieved, but still plenty unhappy.

He hopped out of the truck and strode to Darla's window. "Where have you been?"

"What?" she said, while Jackie stared at him, almost gawking. "What do you mean, where have I been?"

Judah tried to cool his jets so his blood pressure wouldn't pop out of his head like a fountain. "You scared me. I didn't know where you were."

Darla blinked big blue eyes at him. "I had my two-week doctor's appointment, Judah. Goodness."

"Oh." Sheepishly, he stepped away from the window, and the mirth in Jackie's eyes. "Sorry about that. Hi, Jackie. Thanks for driving Darla."

"Hi, Judah," Jackie said. "Mind moving your truck so I can get by?"

"I'm going." Okay, he was going to be the laughingstock of the town. He'd just made a superior ass of himself. He backed up, parked, then followed the ladies to the house. They didn't pay a whole lot of attention to him as they went inside. Darla slowly seated herself on the sofa, and Jackie got her a glass of ice water.

"I'm going now," Jackie said to Judah. "Think you can handle it from here?"

"Yes," he said, his tone gruff, his gaze drinking in his tired wife. "Thanks, Jackie."

"No problem. She has another appointment in a couple of weeks, so put that on your calendar so you don't give yourself a coronary." His sister-in-law smiled at him and waved goodbye to Darla as she popped out the door.

"Sorry," Judah said. "I've lost my mind."

Darla sighed. "I didn't think to tell you because it wasn't important."

"Yeah." He took a seat beside his wife. "I won't always be like this. I don't think so, anyway."

"You won't," Darla said, "or I'll put you back in the pond, toad."

"Speaking of ponds," Judah said, "Fiona told me you might be looking for a new one."

She closed her eyes, leaning her head back. "It's as good a time as any, I suppose."

"I thought we talked about the fact that you're not supposed to be doing anything, not even so much as moving one of those tiny, pink-painted piggies of yours," he said with a frown.

"Judah, I only made a phone call. I didn't lift weights or pull a truck." Darla sighed. "Are you always going to be difficult and overbearing? Because I'm not sure I saw this side of you when I let you sweep me off my feet."

"Who swept who?" He brought her hand to his lips and kissed it, then took the plunge. "Are you thinking about moving out to the ranch?" He ran a lock of her silver-blond hair between his fingers, mesmerized by the silkiness of it, as he waited for her to give him the answer he wanted so badly.

"I've always wanted to live in a renovated bunkhouse," Darla said.

"Have you really?" Judah asked, and she said, "No. But I'm willing to give it a shot."

He grinned, the happiest man on earth. "Thank you," he said. "If you're sure."

She rolled her head to look at him. "I'm not completely sure."

"Oh." He didn't know what to make of that. He just knew he'd feel better if she was at the ranch, where more eyes could be on her, and on his daughters.

"But I've always been practical." She gazed at him. "Something tells me my downside risk is minimal."

"Can I have your cell number now that I've talked you into moving into a run-down bunkhouse with me?" he said, and Darla smiled.

"Exchanging cell numbers seems like a very serious step."

He kissed her nose. "Commitment is fun. You'll see."

THE NEXT MORNING, Judah was feeling slightly better about things. He and Darla had spent a pleasant evening together, even sleeping in the same room. It was a milestone for him. He was becoming less afraid of hurting her, and the future seemed pretty rosy. One small step at a time, baby steps, he told himself, whistling as he went to the barn. *And soon my babies will be coming home, too.*

"Hey, did you hear the big news?" Sam asked from the barn office. Jonas and Rafe were sitting in there with him. They all wore half-moon grins.

Judah paused. "I never hear any news. What's the news flash?"

They all laughed, practically waiting to pounce on him *en masse.*

"That you got your wife's cell phone number!" Sam said, guffawing like a pirate. "You're really slick now, bro."

Rafe nodded. "Jackie told us all about it. She said you were in a panic when she brought Darla home from her appointment yesterday. That you were breathing like a woman in labor."

"I was not." Judah slung his hat onto the desk. "I just...I mean, what the hell was I supposed to think?"

"We're just ribbing you. The news is that Sidney and Diane eloped," Jonas said.

"What?" Judah's jaw went slack.

"Yep," Sam said. "Just think, if Sidney had married Darla,

he'd probably have had her cell number by now. But that's okay. We're not embarrassed by you or anything. Every family's got its runt in the love department."

"No one has to tell me that the small details have been known to get by me." Judah looked at his brothers. "Is this good news about Sidney and Diane?"

They all shrugged.

"It's not bad news," Sam said. "It's just news."

"I guess." Judah sank onto a chair. "But it's so fast."

"Maybe for you," Rafe said. "But not every man is frightened of women."

"I am not—oh, hell. Why do I bother?" He was a little afraid of Darla, he supposed. He definitely had her on a high pedestal, keeping her out of reach. "I don't feel like I'm standing in knee-deep mud. It feels like I'm running pretty fast."

"But you're not getting anywhere." Sam nodded. "We understand. We're trying to help you."

"I don't need any help." Judah got up. "We get plenty of help. More than we need."

"But Sidney bagged his female and is off on a beach in Hawaii, while you're making your wife move into a little-used bunkhouse," Rafe said. "We think your romance quotient is low. We've been theorizing about where you went wrong."

"I haven't," Judah said, heading off to the stalls, wondering if he had gone wrong, when he wanted everything to be so right.

Chapter Nineteen

"So the ballistics showed that the bullet was from a .38," Fiona told Judah as she swept out the bunkhouse. "Sheriff Cartwright doesn't think it was a random hunter's bullet."

"I could have figured that." Judah watched his little aunt getting the bunkhouse ready for his brood to take over. "What can I do to help?"

"Stay out of my way," Fiona said cheerfully. "I think I'm going to have to take down these red-and-white gingham curtains. They're too bunkhousey for a new family. I know Darla will want to decorate your home, but she doesn't have any time right now, and this can all be changed later. So I think we'll do plain white lace curtains Darla can replace."

Judah helped his aunt move some furniture. "You work too hard. Let me have that broom."

"You just take care of your arm. Don't think I haven't noticed that you bark at Darla but haven't exactly been taking care of yourself."

He shrugged. "It was a scratch."

Fiona sighed. "Judah, remember when you found the cave?"

"Yeah." He pushed the furniture back and waited for Fiona's broom to land in a new spot so he could try to help her. "If you tell me what needs cleaning, I can do this, Aunt Fiona."

"You're not paying attention." She wrapped a rag on the end of the broom and gestured to the overhead fans for him to dust. "You didn't mention the cave to anyone, did you?"

"No. Not even my daughters, whom I spend every waking moment with when I'm not with my wife." He grinned. "They're making good progress. And the doc says in a month or so they'll be over five pounds and can come home."

His aunt smiled. "Maybe home will be here, if Darla doesn't change her mind."

"Why would she?" He frowned but didn't look at Fiona as he dutifully moved the broom around the wagon wheel chandeliers and fans.

"I don't know." She watched him with an eagle eye to make certain no dust was missed. "Anyway, if we can keep to one subject, Burke and I have been talking it over, and we think there's possibly a connection between you getting shot and the cave."

Just talking about it was making his arm hurt. Or maybe reaching for dust and cobwebs was doing that. Judah ignored the pain and kept dusting, wanting everything perfect for Darla. He was so happy she was willing to live here that he could hardly stand it. And then, in time, he'd build her the house of her dreams.

Their family would begin here, at Rancho Diablo.

"Did you hear me?" Fiona asked, and Judah snapped his thoughts away from Darla.

"Yes, dear aunt. You said the cave is the reason I got shot. But that makes no sense, because Bode doesn't know about the cave, and he wouldn't shoot me at my own wedding, anyway." He handed the broom back to his aunt. "Clean enough even for a nurse."

Fiona looked at him. "Bode didn't do it."

She had his full attention now. "How do you know?"

"A feeling I have."

Judah snorted. "You don't act on feelings. You've always been too practical for anything but data and hard evidence. Even when we were kids, you didn't believe anything you heard about us until you saw proof that we'd painted a neighbor's goat for the Fourth of July, or that we'd been smoking in the fields outside of town."

Fiona's lips went flat. "If I'd believed every rumor I'd heard about you kids, you would have been doing chores for the rest of your lives."

Judah shrugged. "So it makes no sense that you'd be dealing in hunches now."

"Except that it's not really a hunch. There are things I can't tell you—"

"Why?" Judah demanded. "We're all full-grown men, Aunt Fiona, not little boys. You don't have to bear the burden of protecting us any longer."

"I know." She nodded. "I'll tell you eventually, as soon as I know the time is right. And I know that time is coming very soon. I knew it the night you got shot."

"I just don't understand what it has to do with the cave. I know someone would love to help himself to the silver. But why pick me?" He looked at her for a moment. "Because I found it and whoever it was didn't want me to?"

She didn't say anything. Judah's blood began to run cold. "You're not trying to tell me that Darla and the girls might be in danger, are you?"

"I don't know," Fiona said. "I didn't expect anyone to try to harm you. Frankly, I'm scared to death."

He sank onto the old sofa in front of a fireplace that hadn't been used in years. "What does Burke say?"

"That you should be careful," Fiona said simply. "We don't know what we're up against now."

"But it has nothing to do with Bode trying to run us off."

She shook her head. "We think Bode is the type of man

who tries to buy everything he wants, or cheat people of it, but he wouldn't kill anybody. I know I cracked him with my bag that night, but once I cooled down, I realized how unlike him it would be to use foul means. He's too much about the thrill of destruction. He likes being able to take people down legally, and sometimes a little bit under the law. I'm not saying he'd bring us a loaf of bread if we were starving. He'd enjoy watching a family be run off. But he wouldn't physically harm any of us. He wouldn't want Julie to see him in a bad light."

"So you're telling me I'm bringing my wife and kids here, and we have a murderer running around?" Anger assailed Judah as he thought of what he would do if anybody ever tried to harm Darla and the babies.

For the first time, he knew he was capable of harming another human. And it scared him. But he knew he would protect his family at all costs. It made him keenly aware of how Fiona must have felt all these years about the family for which she'd been responsible.

"We were at Darla's for your wedding that night," she said softly, reminding him. "We weren't here."

His throat went dry; blood pounded in his ears. "You're right. I've always thought of Rancho Diablo as the unsafe place because of Bode." But Fiona was correct. Whoever shot him—if it had been on purpose—had followed him to his own wedding, a time when he would have had his guard down completely. It felt like a warning.

"Darla's alone at the house," Judah said, and ran for his truck.

DARLA LET OUT A SCREECH when the back door crashed open. As Judah burst into the living room, she wanted to bash him with the baby name book she was holding. "What in the world, Judah?"

He slowed down, his eyes crazy, his dark hair blown and

wild around his head. He was, unfortunately, handsome as all get-out, but she wanted to slap him silly. Maybe she would as soon as her heart slowed down.

"What are you doing?" he demanded.

"What does it look like I'm doing? I'm trying to pick baby names. For heaven's sake, Judah, you frightened me!" She glared at him. "I thought we talked about this. You were going to calm down." She worked herself up into some righteous anger. "You just can't keep acting like a madman. You've been crazy ever since you found out I was pregnant, and it's only gotten worse." She bit her lip, then said, "Or maybe I never really knew you."

"Of course we didn't know each other," Judah replied. "I could never get you to even talk to me."

"Well, I'm talking now, and I swear, if you don't calm down..." She looked at him. "Why did you come in here like you were running from the devil, anyway? What is your problem?"

He put his good arm around her, holding her. She could feel his heart beating hard in his chest, ricocheting in panic. "What is wrong with you, Judah?"

"I don't know," he said. "Actually, I do know, but some things are better left unsaid."

She pushed him away and went to stare at him from the sofa. "I don't know that I can live with a crazy man. You literally frightened me out of my wits. I didn't know who was coming in the house." She frowned at him. "Why did you use the back door, anyway?"

"I overshot the driveway," he said, a little embarrassed. "So I came in the rear. I was in a hurry." He gathered her to him once more, ignoring his wounded arm. "I worry about you, I guess. And did you know that Sidney and Diane eloped?"

She pushed him away a final time and said sternly, "The driveway is not a speedway. You nearly hit Jackie's truck the other day." Darla gave him a long look, thinking it was a shame that her handsome husband had such race car driver tendencies. "Look. Is there anything I can do to make you feel less insane?"

"I don't think so," Judah said. "I think it's the new me."

She sighed, trying to be patient, which wasn't easy. "You can't be jealous if Sidney and Diane have eloped, so what's bugging you now?"

He shrugged. "I wouldn't say I'm done being jealous of ol' Sid. Sometimes I wonder what women see in that bony bronc buster. But as far as what's bugging me, it's not Tunstall. I haven't figured everything out yet, to be honest. It's a work in progress."

"So maybe you're always going to be a fat-headed ass?" Darla was in no mood to let him off the hook. "You're going to have to get a grip."

He would, but not today. He'd been a dad for only four days—and as far as he was concerned, he had over a month to change. He could do it. "Keep the faith, wife."

ON THE FIRST OF AUGUST, Judah could honestly say that "Coming Home Day" was the best day of his life. "Miss Jennifer Belle Callahan," he said proudly, laying daughter number one gently in her bassinet, "and Miss Molly Mavis Callahan." He placed his second daughter near her sister in a matching bassinet.

Instantly, both babies began to cry. "They don't like their names," Judah said, feeling helpless.

"They want to be together." Darla sat up in bed and motioned for him to hand her his daughters. Gingerly, as if he was handling small, fragile pieces of china, he passed the girls one by one to their mother. Darla made sure their blankets were wrapped properly, then put the girls side by side next to her on the bed. Instantly, they stopped fussing, and Judah's nerves stopped jumping.

"I don't like it when I don't know what they want."

"You'll learn. We'll learn. Right now, I'm sure the girls just want to feel like they did in the womb."

He nodded. "Looks good to me. Any room for Dad?"

"Come on." Darla motioned to the other side of the twins.

"I don't know," Judah said, hanging back. "I read that it was bad for Dad to sleep in the bed with babies."

"It might be, but you're not going to sleep," Darla said. "I haven't seen you sleep for weeks. Do you ever?"

He thought about it. "Now that you mention it, I don't think so."

Darla smiled. "Just don't roll over on them, and everybody will be happy."

He stared down, wanting very much to get in but not sure it was safe. The bed seemed so big, for one thing. And it was full of females. While this was normally a good thing, these females were all in a very delicate state. "I think I'll wait until everyone is a little more, uh, ready for company," he said, backing away. "I'll sit over here in the rocker and watch you ladies enjoy having the bed to yourselves. It won't last forever, so take advantage of it while you can."

Darla shook her head at him. "You're afraid of your daughters."

"Sometimes I'm afraid of you. I'm not ashamed to admit that." Judah waved his hand and then reached for a pink baby blanket to roll up behind his head. "The guy who can't admit the truth isn't much of a man."

"That's nice. Did you make that up?" Darla asked. "I've never known the philosophizing side of you."

He yawned. "I think so. Then again, I might have plagiarized it from somebody smarter than me."

And then he fell asleep.

Darla looked at her knocked-out husband and smiled tenderly down at her babies. "He's going to be better now, I think, girls. Bringing you home was the best thing that could happen to him." It was true. The moment he'd held his daughters and brought them home, she'd sensed a change in him. He wasn't frantic or rattled up anymore.

Judah seemed content.

Darla kissed each of her daughters on the head, falling in love with all the new people in her life, and the magic she could feel binding them together as a family.

WHEN JUDAH OPENED his eyes, he found Darla and the babies gone. Pushing himself out of the rocker, he went to find his family. They were quietly nursing on the sofa in the den, and he was amazed that he'd apparently slept through baby calls for breakfast. "Sorry. I guess I was tired. What can I do to help?"

"Hold a baby," Darla said with a smile, and he thought he'd never seen her look more beautiful. He found himself literally gawking at his wife.

"I want to marry you," he said, and Darla laughed.

"We are married."

"I know. But I'm afraid you'll get away from me. Maybe I'll marry you once a month just to make sure you're holding tight to our commitment." He sank onto the sofa and trailed a finger over his daughter's face as she nuzzled her mom. "Remember when you used to talk about our marriage as something you wanted to do until the girls were born?"

Darla nodded. "Is that what's making you all nervous and weird?"

"No, this is my natural state now," he said, and she nodded.

"Probably." She handed him the daughter who'd gone to sleep on her breast.

"So," he said, taking the baby tenderly, "if you don't mind,

I'd like to make this a solid, no-holds-barred commitment. I have a feeling you're going to like being married to me."

Darla laughed. "Well, confidence isn't your short suit."

"So, I'll go rustle up some breakfast. What are you in the mood for, little mama?" The least he could do was grab some grub, since she was doing all the work—and as lovely as that work was, she didn't seem to need him all that much.

"Fruit," Darla said. "I'd kiss you for fresh fruit."

"Really? Does a truckload rate more than a kiss?"

Darla smiled at him, and Judah tried to ignore the fact that she hadn't said a whole lot about staying married to him longer than the time it took to give his daughters his name.

Which was now.

"Oh, that reminds me," he said, "speaking of gifts and whatnot—"

"We weren't," she said. "We were just talking about breakfast."

"Well, I know, but a guy has to work in opportunity when it presents itself." He handed her the jeweler's box he'd picked up in town. "It's not a banana or an apple, but it's something."

She indicated the baby on her breast she was supporting with one arm. "Would you mind opening it for me? My hands are full at the moment."

Okay, so maybe his timing wasn't all that great. Judah told himself it didn't matter—timing wasn't everything.

Or maybe it was. He snapped open the lid, and Darla gasped.

"Judah!"

He laughed when she freed a hand to grab the box so she could look at the sapphire bracelet more closely.

"It's gorgeous," she said. "But what's it for?"

He chuckled and took the box back. "To thank you for my babies? To work my way out of the doghouse I land myself in occasionally? I don't know. Maybe it's because I love you."

She looked at him, cornflower-blue eyes assessing him. "Do you?"

"I might," he said, putting the sapphire-and-diamond bracelet on her wrist. "Maybe. When you're ready."

She looked at the bracelet, then smiled. "Thank you. It's the most beautiful thing I've ever owned."

"I don't know about that." Judah stroked his daughter's tiny head. "Our babies look like their mom. So they are the most beautiful things I own."

Darla's eyes sparkled, and then she broke eye contact. "Thank you," she murmured.

"You're welcome. So," he said cheerfully, feeling better about his place in the world already. "Bananas? Apples? Peaches?"

"All," she said, looking back at him, "and when does the moving truck arrive?"

Chapter Twenty

"About that moving truck," Judah said. "I think it's too soon, don't you?"

Darla touched the lovely bracelet he had given her, and wondered why he was so worried about every little thing. She was fine; their daughters were fine. He'd asked her about making a real commitment, and that commitment was best made in a home they started out in together. Maybe Rancho Diablo was just so much a part of him that he couldn't relax until he was there.

"If you're worried about me, Judah, don't be. I've waited a long time for us to be a family. You don't have to stress out all the time."

"I do," Judah said. "It's a new husband, new dad thing."

"All right," Darla said. "But the sooner you're not feeling like a fish out of water, the sooner you'll de-stress."

"I don't know. I'm accepting stress as my due in life at the moment. But," he said, clearly trying to take all the blame for his unease, "I would feel better at the ranch, although not for the reason you assume. I'm not unhappy here with you, Darla. If things were different, this house would be fine for a month or two. At least until our daughters start needing some elbow room."

Darla gazed down at their diminutive babies. "I think that'll be a while, don't you?"

"Nah. They're going to be tall like their mother and father."

"That's probably true, but I don't think it'll happen overnight."

"The way they're chowing, I wouldn't underestimate them," Judah said enviously, eyeing his breast-feeding daughter.

Darla smiled. "So what's the reason?"

"What reason?" He appeared momentarily disoriented from staring at her breasts, and Darla shook her head.

"The real reason you want to move to the ranch, if it isn't for a bigger house to raise your family in."

"Oh," Judah said, bringing his gaze back to her eyes. "I don't know."

She frowned. "Yes, you do. You're a pretty practical guy. You know why you do things. So quit hiding it."

"Uh, I have to get breakfast for my love right now," he said, edging toward the door. "Don't you worry about a thing while I'm gone, and when I get back, I'll watch babies so you can shower."

He escaped out the door, and a second later she heard his truck roar off down the driveway, no slower than he'd driven in. He was always in a hurry. Darla looked down at the bracelet on her arm, mesmerized by the twinkling diamonds and deep blue sapphires, and wondered why Judah wouldn't just tell her what he was thinking.

"Maybe he's one of those men who keep everything inside," she murmured to her daughters. "The strong, silent type. Which will be hard to deal with since I'm not a mind reader."

She knew he'd wanted her out at the ranch yesterday—but he'd just said it wasn't because of building their life together in a bigger house. Darla closed her eyes after a moment, deciding to relax and not think about her mysterious man. Judah was Judah—and he moved to a drummer that only he seemed to be able to hear.

"WELL, LOOK AT YOU, making the doughnut run," Bode Jenkins said as Judah loaded the groceries he'd grabbed onto the checkout counter. Bode glanced over his purchases. "Hungry wife?"

Judah grunted. "Bode, mind your own business."

"Hey, that's no way to talk to a neighbor."

Judah ignored the comment, paid his bill with cash and departed. Bode followed, trying to keep up with Judah's long strides.

"I mean to give you a wedding gift," the older man stated, and Judah said, "Don't bother."

"Callahan," Bode said, his voice changing to a more insistent tone, "you really ought to be nicer to me."

"Why?" Judah asked. "Nice really isn't my deal, but most especially not to you. And I don't have time to chat this morning, Bode. If you have a complaint with me, lodge it with someone who cares." He got in his truck, tossing the groceries on the seat next to him.

Bode stood at the window. "Listen, I think I know who shot you."

Judah hesitated in the act of turning on the engine, surprised that Bode had brought up the shooting, and wondering if he should even bother to listen to anything the old man had to say. "If you think you know, why don't you tell the sheriff?"

"Wouldn't you rather I tell you?"

Judah scrubbed at his morning growth of beard, wishing he had a magic club he could beat Bode over the head with and make him disappear. "Jenkins, if you knew anything at all you'd be shouting it from the rooftops, not trying to keep me from my family when you can see I'm on a mission." He started the truck. "To be honest, I don't care who shot me. You can't scare us off our land, Jenkins. Callahans don't scare."

"It involves your aunt, and some other things I think you'd be interested in."

"All right," Judah said, "spit it out so I can get home to my hungry wife and kids."

"Ask your aunt," Bode advised, and Judah said, "What?"

"Ask your aunt who likely shot you."

"Jump, Jenkins," Judah said, "'cause this truck door'll swing open in two seconds and knock you flat to the ground."

Bode jumped away from the vehicle and Judah drove off, swearing under his breath. He cursed colorfully, using words he rarely said, and told himself it was against the law to back up over an old man, even if Bode deserved it. Judah pressed the pedal down, peeling out of the parking lot, eager to get home. Never had he been more anxious to see his wife and children.

DARLA HEARD JUDAH'S TRUCK roar up the drive, and was mentally ready when the front door blew open with a great sucking sound. "Shh," she said, "the babies are asleep, Attila."

"Attila?" Judah handed her the bag of fruit. "Who's he?"

"He was a man who was always on a conquering mission. You've just about conquered my driveway and my door frames. I'm going to need to have everything Judah-proofed."

"Sorry," he said, and she sighed.

"You were going to start acting like a human being?"

He shrugged. "Maybe it takes a while."

"Hmm." Darla went to the kitchen and got out plates. "Thank you for the fruit. It's beautiful."

"Babies are beautiful." Judah threw himself onto the sofa, looking rattled even for him, Darla thought. "Fruit is just appetizing. Or not."

She shook her head and cut the fruit into two bowls. "Are you all right?"

"Yeah." He got up, went to her fridge. "Any beer in here?"

Darla's eyes widened. "At eight o'clock in the morning?"

"Maybe just a fruit chaser." He found a Dos and opened it gratefully.

"That's older than you want, like from a picnic last summer. How about some coffee instead?"

"I'm jacked enough already." He opened the beer and took a swig, made a face and sucked down another swig before pouring the rest down the drain. "That was just what the doctor ordered."

Darla shook her head and handed him a bowl of fruit. "Are you all right?"

"Never been better," Judah said, but Darla had the strangest feeling he wasn't being honest.

And it wasn't the first time she'd felt this way.

She heard a tiny cry from one of the babies, and set her bowl down.

"I got it," Judah said. "Eat."

She hung back in the kitchen as he'd told her to. It would be all right. Judah would call her if he needed help. No sound came from the other room. She chewed her fruit halfheartedly, listening, and when she still heard nothing, she peeked around the corner.

Judah had both babies on his chest as he lounged on the sofa. He peered down one baby's back, hooked a finger in her diaper and peeked. "Nothing there, Dad," he said, talking for the baby, then hooked a finger in the second diaper. "Nothing here, either, Dad," he said, still being a baby ventriloquist.

Darla smiled and brought him his bowl. "What do you know about changing diapers?"

"Just that it needs to happen often or everybody's unhappy." Judah smoothed a hand over tiny heads. "And I did a lot of babysitting in high school. Fiona was a big believer in us working whatever odd job came our way. Babysitting, wrangling, bush hogging. Didn't matter. She said it was good for us to respect a buck."

Darla didn't know where to put herself. She wanted to sit next to Judah, but something held her back. "If you're good with the girls, would you mind if I grab a shower?"

"Go. The babies and I are going to watch an educational flick." He turned on her television, flipped channels with the remote and chose the movie download. "For our first foray into intelligentsia," he told his daughters, "we're going to examine the societal differences between *Little Women* and *Gone with the Wind.* I'll expect spirited discussion during intermissions."

Darla laughed. "Oh, you'll get spirited discussions, but they'll all be concerning dinner."

"Switch out the lights, please. We must have the proper surroundings to begin the study of our topic of females in society."

"Okay," Darla said. "By the way, your aunt will be here in thirty minutes."

"Why?"

"You'll see," Darla said with a smile, and left the room.

"When you become literary bra burners," Judah told his daughters, "please remind yourselves that men don't like surprises." He said it loudly enough for Darla to hear in the next room, and she rewarded him by saying, "Men like spice, girls. Never forget the spice."

And then Darla put tape on the final packed box in her room, sealing it and marking it "Darla and Judah's bedroom."

We'll see how well my husband handles surprises.

THIRTY MINUTES LATER, Judah had just gotten comfortable watching *Little Women* when the door banged open.

"We're here!" Jonas called out. "Darla, we're here!"

"Hi," Fiona said, poking her head into the living room. "What are you doing here, Judah?"

His brothers and Burke piled in behind Fiona.

"Have you guys ever heard of being quiet so as not to wake sleeping babies?" Judah said with a growl.

"Not those two. They sleep like puppies." Fiona came to kiss each great-niece on her downy head.

"Anyway, what do you mean, what am I doing here?" Judah didn't appreciate the inference that he might not be where his wife and daughters were.

"Well," Sam said, "we thought you'd be off doing something stupid, like trying to solve the universe's problems. We're trying to give you a surprise party."

"Party?" Judah raised a brow. "What kind of surprise party? I don't like surprises."

"And yet it's been one after another for the past several months. Good morning, girls," Rafe said, touching a palm to each of his niece's tufts. "Miss me?"

"No, they don't," Judah said. "We are trying to have a literary discussion."

"Oh, your favorite movie." Jonas laughed, and when Darla came into the living room he told her, "Judah always wanted to be Laurie."

"Didn't happen, though," Sam said. "Judah was never polite enough to be Laurie."

"True. He's been a little on the crabby side lately." Darla smiled, and Fiona said, "Are we ready?"

"Everything is boxed up." Darla took them back to her room, and Judah tried to spy down the hall to see what they were doing. He couldn't move the two tiny bundles on his chest, however, because they were so warm and satisfied right where they were.

"What's happening?" he demanded as Burke went by with a wheeled dolly.

"We're moving your wife and girls to the ranch," Jonas said. "Surprise!"

Chapter Twenty-One

Once they had Darla and Molly and Belle moved into the bunkhouse, Judah really did feel peace come over him. There were so many people coming and going all day long at Rancho Diablo that he knew his ladies were safe.

Which meant it was time to talk to Fiona. He caught her heading to the basement, her favorite haunt besides the kitchen. "Whoa, frail aunt, let me carry those for you."

She sniffed and gave him the box of party lights she'd hung in June. "I'm not frail. You're frail."

"In what way?"

"You're making your wife do all the heavy lifting."

He stared at Fiona as they made their way down the stairs. "What lifting?"

"She's making all the sacrifices."

It was true. "Not much I can do about that right now."

"You could take her on a honeymoon. Let me keep the babies."

He hesitated. "Uh, she's breast-feeding."

"True, but trips aren't planned in a week, nephew. Good ones, at least. There are logistics involved. And I'll probably have to fight Mavis tooth and nail for baby time, so I want to get my request in first."

She sniffed again, and Judah said, "Catching a cold, Aunt?"

"No. I'm merely allergic to bone idleness."

"I suppose you have the name of a travel agency you prefer?" he asked with a sigh.

"I do. But I refuse to pick a destination. You'll have to ask Darla what she wants. I can't do everything for you."

He smiled. "Thanks for thinking of it. I'd forgotten."

"You've had a lot on your mind." She showed him where to shove the box, and pointed to another she wanted.

"I thought you were going to have a monster garage sale and get rid of all this."

"I might, if we ever have to move. But right now, Sam's doing a bang-up job. I'm only fifty percent worried these days. And Jonas has become quite the financial investor, something I was never aware of before. Guess he has to have something to do now that he's not cracking open people's chest cavities."

Judah winced. "Aunt, speaking of cracking things open..."

"Oh, let's don't," she said. "I hate to think of it. Only eggs should be cracked open."

His gaze slid to the dirt patch that was unlike the rest of the basement floor. They'd asked Fiona about it when they were younger, and gotten some water-seeping-in, covered-over-mold story. The boys had told each other ghost stories about the dead body in the basement, but these days, Judah wondered if he could dismiss any tale about his fey aunt.

"What about safes? Safes get cracked open."

"No," she said dismissively, "not unless one is a thief, and we have none of—" Her gaze met his, and then slid to the floor where he'd been looking. "Now, nephew," Fiona said. "Don't go odd on me just because you're lacking sleep due to your darling daughters. In fact, you should go—"

"Bode says I should ask you about who might have shot me," Judah said quietly, and Fiona stared at him.

"Bode's a fool. Why would he say such a thing?"

"You tell me."

She put her hands on her hips and glared at him. "Whose side are you on, Judah?"

"Callahan side, ma'am," he answered, "but why are there sides?"

She pursed her lips. "I always think of everything that's happened as Jenkins versus Callahan. That's all I meant."

"Do you have a theory as to who shot me?" Judah was determined to know just how much Fiona was hiding.

"I have theories," she said, "and they're about as good as any that are floating around. I've had people ask me if you accidentally let your own gun go off."

"Why would I be carrying at a wedding?"

"See how much sense it makes to listen to gossip?" She moved to inspect her rows of pickled vegetables, breaking eye contact. "I've heard that it was Bode. That it was a hunter. That it was Sidney." She shrugged. "We're probably never going to know, Judah."

And yet he sensed she was holding back on him.

"And who else might it have been?"

She looked at him for a long time. "Put those boxes on the dining room table, please," she said, and marched up the stairs, leaving him in the basement, knowing that something wasn't adding up.

"TONIGHT'S FAMILY COUNCIL is necessary," Fiona said, "because lately I've noticed a lack of faith among my nephews in the job I've been doing. Not that I blame you, because I alone got us in the mess we're in."

The six brothers and Burke watched Aunt Fiona as she struggled for words six hours after Judah had tried to talk to her about Bode down in the basement. Of course, he'd known that Bode was intent on stirring up trouble. Yet it was his aunt's lack of heat in the denial that had sparked his curiosity.

Now she was calling a family council, and his curiosity was even greater. They had these meetings at least once a month to discuss family and ranch business, but this one had been called out of schedule.

Now they sat in the wood-paneled library. Burke passed out square cut-crystal glasses of fine whiskey, and Judah drank his gratefully.

"First, Burke and I want to tell you that we're married," Fiona said, "just so you know that I'm walking the walk and talking the talk when I try to set you boys up for lifetimes of happiness with someone you love. I know you already know, have known for a while, but I'm making it official."

The men applauded, congratulated Burke and Fiona, acted surprised, as if they hadn't figured it out years ago.

"Now I'm here to answer any questions you might have," Fiona said, "and I know that, based on a discussion I had with Judah this morning, that you have some. Anything we can clear up, Burke and I are here for you. Always."

The brothers glanced at one another. This was new, Judah thought. This new transparent Fiona was an unexpected metamorphosis.

And yet she'd specifically told him never to talk about the cave's existence. He wondered how far this transparency would go.

"All right, I'll bite," Judah said. "Where are our parents buried?"

The room went deathly silent. Fiona's gaze leveled on him, seemingly dazed, and then, without any warning, she fainted.

"SHE SCARED THE LIVING daylights out of me," Judah said as he lay in bed that night with Darla and their two angels. "I really thought I'd killed her."

Darla giggled. "It's not funny, I know, but it kind of is. You know Fiona is tough as cowhide. I don't think you can hurt her, Judah. Don't worry."

He winced. "I do worry. She's not so much cowhide as she once was. I feel terrible about the whole thing." His brothers had piled on, telling him that Fiona's offer had been more rhetorical and polite than anything, and was he trying to give her a stroke?

"Don't worry. Fiona knows you love her." Darla gave a contented sigh. "I love living in this bunkhouse," she said, and Judah's attention was totally caught.

"Are you being serious?"

She nodded. "Much more than I thought I would. It's really ideal for a growing family. There's so much storage space. And Mom and her friends came over today and set up the nursery just the way they had it at my house." She smiled at Judah. "It's perfect."

"I'm glad." His tone was gruffer than he meant it to be, but so much emotion was flooding over him that it practically choked him. "Thanks for being okay with this, Darla. I feel better with us being here."

"Yeah, Sam told me." Darla closed her eyes, enjoying the peace. "He said that ever since you got shot, you've been a bit of a wienie."

Judah sighed. "He's probably right."

"And he said that this is your place. Your piece of the universe." She rolled her head to look at him. "I didn't really have a piece of the universe. I loved my house, but it was just a house."

You're my home, he thought, *my whole life. My real universe.*

"Want to honeymoon?" he asked, and Darla grinned at him.

"MAYBE THE BAHAMAS," Darla told Jackie the next day when she came to see the new digs and bring a housewarming gift.

"Judah says I can probably find a white skirt and he'll wear a white shirt with palm trees on it, and we'll have vows said under some kind of coconut tree or something." Darla smiled. "He's gone all romantic since we moved into the bunkhouse."

"Rancho Diablo suits these men." Jackie pulled out wedding dress vendor photos for two years out. "I figure we might as well start looking these over."

"And I need to decide what to do with the magic wedding dress," Darla said. "I suppose we should sell it. Sabrina says the magic has to keep moving."

"Do you really believe all that stuff she talks about sometimes?"

"I don't know," Darla said, "but I do know that I'm happier than I've ever been, and if a dress can bring a little luck, I'm all for sharing it. I'm a romantic at heart."

"So am I." Jackie looked at the photos and drawings. "You're still okay with the wedding dress shop, partner?"

"Why wouldn't I be?" Darla was surprised by the question.

"I thought Judah didn't want you to work."

"Well, not while the babies are so tiny." Darla stiffened. "I didn't mind changing houses, but I would never give up my shop for a man. Not Judah or any other guy."

"Just checking."

Darla frowned, not sure where all this was going. "You've got triplets, so why wouldn't I keep working, too?"

Jackie shrugged. "Pete doesn't mind me working."

Darla wondered if Judah cared if she worked. If he did, he was going to get a fat lip. "This dress shop was my brainchild, and I wouldn't give it up for him. I don't think he'd ask, either."

Jackie nodded. "I was pretty certain you'd feel that way."

Tickles of unease ran over Darla. "You're not telling me everything. What happened?"

Jackie sighed. "Judah came to me and offered to buy out my half of the shop."

"What?" Darla couldn't believe what she was hearing. "Why?"

"Well, Pete says Judah was planning on giving it to you as a wedding gift."

Darla thought about that. "But I don't want to own the whole store. I like the way we have things set up." She frowned. "How dare he?"

"I think Judah has your best interests at heart, Darla," Jackie said calmly. Her efforts to soothe her weren't working, however, because Darla was practically quivering with anger.

"Why?" she asked her friend. "Why do you think that?"

Jackie's face wore a how-do-I-get-myself-out-of-this expression. "Pete says if you own the whole store, you can sell it and have more time for the babies."

Darla began to quiver again. "I haven't even thought that far ahead. Why would Judah think he has to be involved in my business?"

"Because he's a man, and because he's a Callahan, and because he honestly thinks he's doing the right thing."

"By thinking for me?" Darla soothed Molly and Belle, who were beginning to get restless from the angry tone of their mother's voice.

"He says he doesn't want you too tired out." Jackie nodded. "And you know, Darla, when we bought the shop, we were single women, and now we're married with children, and your babies are very delicate—"

"Don't give me that. You don't want to sell your half," Darla said. "I know you too well."

"No, but if it's best for you—"

"It's not," Darla said, her tone dark with finality. "Just forget my husband ever brought this up."

"Oh, dear," Jackie said. "I don't want to cause trouble."

"You didn't. Judah did."

And the moment her man got home, he was going to get his chauvinistic tendencies trimmed way back. There was a difference between diamond-and-sapphire bracelets and buying out one's sister-in-law—a difference her handsome husband was about to learn.

"STORM BREWING TO THE east," Rafe told Judah as they put away the last of the horses. "We'll pull the barn doors shut when we go."

"Okay." Judah glanced over his shoulder at the bruised sky. Winds were swirling the clouds, sending them scudding across the dark heavens. "When's Diane coming back?"

"She and Sidney return tonight. They'll take the girls to their new house in Durant, where Sidney lives." Rafe put his saddle away, and Judah did likewise. "I'm going to miss the heck out of the little girls."

"Whoa," Judah said, an arrow of sadness shooting through him. "I guess I should have expected that." The girls had been going back and forth from Jackie to Fiona to Aberdeen while their mother was gone, with Aberdeen keeping them at night. Still, Judah was going to miss the sound of their young voices.

"It's sad, but nothing stays the same. Eventually, all little birds fly away," Rafe said.

"We didn't."

"Our jobs are here," Rafe reminded him. "But you tried to fly. You just got your wings clipped."

"I think of it more as if I got my wings retooled. They're better now." Judah was proud of how he was handling his new settled life. He couldn't wait for the big All's Clear from the doctor—he was going to make love to his wife until he gave out. "Life's great. You should try marriage."

"Not me," Rafe said. "I don't do relationships."

"Neither did I," Judah said, pretty cheerful about the new him.

"So, about the other night," Rafe said. "What made you ask about our parents?"

He shrugged. "I'd like to know. Wouldn't you?"

"I don't know. I'm a year older than you. I understand that there are some things we'll never know. At twenty-nine, you decide it's too late to know some things."

"When you're looking down the barrel at thirty, you mean?" Judah shook his head. "Not me. I'll always want to know what happened. How did they die? Where were they?"

"They died," Rafe said, "of some funky illness."

"I thought it was a car accident." Judah frowned. "You know, it's not that hard to request a death certificate. Sam probably has done so a thousand times for clients."

Rafe turned to look at him. "Do you think Fiona would have told us, if we really wanted to know?"

"You mean we don't want to?"

Rafe shrugged. "Do you?"

"I—yeah."

"Then order the certificate." Rafe walked out of the barn into the storm, leaving Judah to wonder why he was the only one in the family who asked questions.

Finding out more about the cave was going to be first on his to-do list, Judah thought. After exiting the barn, he turned to slide the doors shut behind him, and suddenly felt a splitting pain in his skull, followed by blackness.

INSIDE THE KITCHEN, Fiona had the entire family scattered about, perching wherever they could find space. "This is our last meal as an extended family," she said over the din, "because tomorrow night our three little ladies go to their new home in Durant. So I cooked their *faborites*—" she stressed the word, imitating the little girls' pronunciation "—SpaghettiO's.

Real sauce and real pasta shaped like Os." She kissed them on their heads. "And now, Judah will lead us in the blessing. Since he's the most newly married, he may have the honor. Judah."

No one said anything. Fiona glanced around the room. "Darla, where's your husband?"

Darla shook her head. "I haven't seen him all day. And if someone does, will you tell him I want to talk to him?"

Everyone hooted at that. Fiona shook her head. "Someone please call his cell phone and tell him it's rude to be late to the little girls' going-away party, especially when their aunty has made them a pink-and-white cake with kitties on it."

"I will." Jonas rang his brother's phone, then said, "No answer. He'll be along soon enough."

Rafe said, "I left him in the barn, so maybe he went to do something else."

Rain pelted the windows. Fiona glanced outside, shaking her head. "All right. I guess we'll eat without him." But she wasn't happy about it.

They were all eating, deep into the spaghetti, when the kitchen door opened. Judah stumbled in, blood running down the side of his face.

Darla screamed and ran to her husband. She waved everyone away as he sank to the floor. "What did you do, Judah?" she asked, grabbing a wet paper towel from Jonas, who hovered near his brother, looking over the wound.

"You've got a mighty big goose egg back here, son," Jonas said. "You're going to need a few stitches. Maybe even a staple. Rafe, check the barn, since you were out there last. Sam, go with him. Look for…look for things," he said, with a quick glance at Fiona.

Judah groaned and slumped toward his wife, and Darla knew at once that everything he'd been worried about had been real. There was trouble, and he didn't want her to know, but was carrying the burden himself.

Her heart grew cold with fear.

"DON'T MOVE," Darla said two hours later, after Jonas brought Judah home from the hospital with a bandage tightly wrapped around his head. "You stay right in that bed. And no TV until I can ascertain that you aren't going to have latent swelling or something. You just sit there and don't move." She was being unreasonable, but she couldn't help being afraid.

"Yes, Nurse," he said. "But will you at least put on a crisp white nurse's uniform with a real short skirt if I have to put up with your bossing me?"

"You're trying to joke about what happened, but it's not funny. First you get shot—"

"Just some kids playing with their daddy's gun, for which they owe me three months' hard labor on the ranch. And I intend to work them harder than my brothers and I ever worked, not to mention mucking. We've got sixteen horses, you know."

She ignored his effort to make light of the situation. "But then you took a knock on the head, and teasing about it just isn't funny right now." She burst into tears.

"And I'm not laughing, either, my love." He patted the bed. "Come over here and let me look down your blouse, and I'll feel ever so much better. The medicine I need is a little naked wife."

Tears streamed faster, so she grabbed a tissue. She hated crying, but couldn't quit. "You scared me!"

"Darling, I scared myself." Judah perked up. "Was it a two-by-four? It felt like a house. Tell me it was at least a really big board."

She nodded. "Sam found it out by the barn. What were you doing, getting in the way of a thick, long piece of lumber?"

"I don't know. Silly of me, wasn't it?"

"Yes! Because you said that if we moved out here, we'd be safer, but clearly you're not!" Darla shrank onto the bed and curled up next to her husband so she could indulge in a little crying on his shoulder. "And you tried to buy Jackie out of her half of the wedding shop, so I really wanted to be angry with you, but now I can't because your head's all bandaged up, so I'm really upset!"

He laughed and tugged her closer. "Now there's the bright side."

She sniffled. "It was horrible when you came into the kitchen all Lon Chaneyish. Never do that again." Darla hiccupped, which she hated to do. But once it got started it always took a while to stop, so she sat next to Judah and hiccupped, aware she sounded pitiful.

"Your daughters aren't as needy as you are," he teased, and Darla stated, "I know. They're angels."

"About the wedding dress shop," Judah began, but she said, "I don't want to fight right now."

"We're not going to fight. I was just trying to buy it for you to help Jackie out. Pete says she's overwhelmed with the triplets right now."

"Oh." Darla thought about that for a few seconds. "Pete told Jackie you were a chauvinist pig who didn't want his wife to work. Not in those words, of course. Those are my words."

"I'll put my brother in the corner with his dunce cap on later. You were really going to tell me off, weren't you?" Judah asked, planting kisses against her hair, and Darla smiled through her tears.

"Yes."

"But since I'm not a chauvinist pig, I get to see you naked for a reward?"

Darla kissed him on the forehead. "The jury's still out on the pig part. Although you're starting to look more like a prince all the time." She got up to go check on the babies, who were nestled in their tiny bassinets.

"Hey," Judah called after her, "what does a guy have to do to prove to his wife that he loves her even when she's not properly dedicated to his nursing care?"

Darla popped her head back in the room. "What did you say?"

"I said..." Judah tried to remember what he'd said that had made Darla return so quickly "...uh, what do I have to do besides take a beating with a two-by-four to get some attention from my wife?"

"Go on," Darla said.

Pain was throbbing at the base of his skull. His long hair had been shaved off in back for the stitches, and his pride was pretty bent about that. Still, Judah tried hard to think. "Oh," he said with a grin, "you're trying to get me tell you that I love you."

"No, I'm not." Darla shook her head. "I'm not trying to get you to *do* anything."

"I love you, Darla," he said. "I loved you long before you ever sneaked into my room and made wild love to me."

"You did?"

She sounded genuinely surprised. Judah nodded, feeling better already. "Why else would I have failed the condom test? I say it was all subconscious."

She advanced on him, her gaze lit with mock anger and a lot of laughter. "When were you going to tell me?"

"When I was certain I'd caught you." He held a pillow in front of himself for protection from his wife. "I love you madly, Darla Callahan, but it was darn hard waiting on you to finally leave your slipper in my path."

She got on top of him, straddling him, and he tossed the pillow away. "Mr. Callahan, are there any other surprises you'd care to share with me?"

He shook his head. "I just want you to know that you're not the only one capable of keeping one's cards to their chest." He gazed at the front of her blouse reverently. "Or breasts, even." He caught one finger in the top and tugged. The blouse fell open, and he sighed with pleasure. "Nurse, I have a terrible ache."

Darla smiled. "I can help you," she said, leaning over to kiss his lips, "but you'll have to undress so I can fix that ache."

He kissed her all over, so passionately that Darla knew she was the luckiest woman on earth. Which was really no surprise at all, because she was married to the man she'd always loved, with all her heart.

Epilogue

"Sheriff says you've had some bad luck," Darla told Judah once they'd taken out the stitches a few weeks later. "He says you shouldn't get in the way of flying boards like that. The storm really kicked up some things."

Shingles had been ripped off the roofs of some houses. Fences had blown down. One of their cows had mysteriously moved onto Bode's property. He'd returned it promptly.

"Don't want you calling me a cattle thief," he'd said, and Fiona had humphed at him.

Judah was glad it was just a board that had hit him, and not one of his brothers, his aunt or his wife. "There are worse things to be in the way of, I guess. Are you packed, wife? Itty bitty bikini and everything?"

Darla laughed. "There will be no bikini. Just a one-piece."

"One-pieces are great. Lots of leg." He rubbed his hands together.

"Did you bring your swimsuit?" Darla asked. "I want to see hunk for the whole week."

He puffed out his chest. "I'm your hunk, darling."

Darla laughed. "Shall we go say goodbye to the girls?"

Judah's face fell. "I'm not sure if I can. I'll miss them too much."

It was true. They were up with him at the crack of dawn when he ate breakfast. He'd make bottles for them, since he'd talked Darla into changing to bottles a bit before their trip. The girls had grown by leaps and bounds. They might have started out slow, but the pediatrician said they were catching up quickly on the growth chart. He said it was amazing. Judah thought it was his wife who was amazing.

Even he was flourishing, living with her.

"When we get this lawsuit settled," he told Darla, "I have a surprise for you."

"Tell me now, just in case," she said, and he grinned at her. "Nah. I like making you beg. It's so much fun."

She swiped at him. "I thought you didn't like surprises."

He swept her into his lap while they waited for Rafe to drive them to the airport. "Well, once I realized surprise was your game, I decided to turn the tables on you."

Darla smiled. "So tell me."

"I'm going to build you your own house."

His wife stared at him for a moment. "Here, at the ranch?"

He nodded. "I don't want to get your hopes up, in case we do lose the ranch."

She kissed him. "I love the bunkhouse, but thank you for thinking of such a wonderful gift. I love you, Judah Callahan."

"I know, Mrs. Callahan. I feel it every day."

"And you know something else?" she said, wrapping her arms around him so she could pull him close, to tell him something she'd long been wanting to tell him, for his ears only. "I had a dream about you last night."

He perked up. "You did? Did it involve naked you and whipped cream and maybe even some cherries?"

She kissed him on the lips. "Even better," she said. "I think we're pregnant."

His jaw dropped.

"Surprise," she said.

Judah laughed and pulled her into his arms, the luckiest, happiest man alive.

When they had put their suitcases in the car, and Rafe was driving them away from Rancho Diablo, Judah saw the Diablos running like the wind, faster than the wind, disappearing on the painted horizon.

And he knew he'd found all the wealth and happiness a man could ever hope for, because the only treasure that truly mattered was love.

* * * * *

There are three Callahan brothers
who have so far eluded the altar!
The stories of Rafe, Sam and Jonas are coming soon.
But first watch for a bonus
Christmas novella—A RANCH DIABLO CHRISTMAS—
coming November 2011 in a special 2-in-1 book,
HOLIDAY IN A STETSON, with Marie Ferrarella!
Only from Harlequin American Romance.